He'd seen the
Janice's eyes.

Someone, or maybe more than someone, had hurt her in some manner in the past.

There were walls...yes, protective walls around her that she'd no doubt carefully constructed, that were bigger and stronger than just a pair of unflattering glasses.

Janice wasn't just keeping men at arm's length; she had the world held at bay, not trusting or believing in anyone who crossed her path.

A surge of hot fury consumed him.

Who had done this to Janice? What exactly had she been subjected to, and when had it happened? He'd like to get his hands on whoever was responsible for hurting her.

And what was it going to take to get Janice to lower those walls of hers, to trust and believe in *him?*

An even more appropriate question was why it mattered so much that Janice knew she could trust him....

Dear Reader,

Summer is a time for backyard barbecues and fun family gatherings. But with all the running around you'll be doing, don't forget to make time for yourself. And there's no better way to escape than with a Special Edition novel. Each month we offer six brand-new romances about people just like you—trying to find the perfect balance between life, career, family, romance....

To start, pick up *Hunter's Woman* by bestselling author Lindsay McKenna. Continuing her riveting MORGAN'S MERCENARIES: THE HUNTERS series, she pairs a strong-willed THAT SPECIAL WOMAN! with the ruggedly handsome soldier who loved her once—and is determined to win her back!

Every woman longs to be noticed for her true beauty—and the heroine of Joan Elliott Pickart's latest book, *The Irresistible Mr. Sinclair*, is no different; this novel features another wonderful hero in the author's exciting cross-line miniseries with Silhouette Desire, THE BACHELOR BET. And for those hankering to return to the beloved Western land that Myrna Temte takes us to in her HEARTS OF WYOMING series, don't miss *The Gal Who Took the West.*

And it's family that brings the next three couples together—a baby on the way in *Penny Parker's Pregnant!* by Stella Bagwell, the next installment in her TWINS ON THE DOORSTEP series that began in Silhouette Romance and will return there in January 2000; adorable twins in Robin Lee Hatcher's *Taking Care of the Twins;* and a millionaire's heir-to-be in talented new author Teresa Carpenter's *The Baby Due Date.*

I hope you enjoy these six emotional must-reads written *by* women like you, *for* women like you!

Sincerely,

Karen Taylor Richman
Senior Editor

Please address questions and book requests to:
Silhouette Reader Service
U.S.: 3010 Walden Ave., P.O. Box 1325, Buffalo, NY 14269
Canadian: P.O. Box 609, Fort Erie, Ont. L2A 5X3

JOAN ELLIOTT PICKART

THE IRRESISTIBLE MR. SINCLAIR

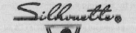

SPECIAL V EDITION®

Published by Silhouette Books
America's Publisher of Contemporary Romance

SILHOUETTE BOOKS

ISBN 0-373-24256-5

THE IRRESISTIBLE MR. SINCLAIR

Copyright © 1999 by Joan Elliott Pickart

Printed in U.S.A.

Books by Joan Elliott Pickart

Silhouette Special Edition

*Friends, Lovers...and
  Babies! #1011
*The Father of Her Child #1025
†Texas Dawn #1100
†Texas Baby #1141
‡Wife Most Wanted #1160
The Rancher and the Amnesiac
  Bride #1204
ΔThe Irresistible Mr.
  Sinclair #1256

Silhouette Desire

*Angels and Elves #961
Apache Dream Bride #999
†Texas Moon #1051
†Texas Glory #1088
Just My Joe #1202
ΔTaming Tall, Dark Brandon #1223

*The Baby Bet
†Family Men
‡Montana Mavericks: Return
  to Whitehorn
ΔThe Bachelor Bet

Previously published under the pseudonym Robin Elliott

Silhouette Special Edition

Rancher's Heaven #909
Mother at Heart #968

Silhouette Intimate Moments

Gauntlet Run #206

Silhouette Desire

Call It Love #213
To Have It All #237
Picture of Love #261
Pennies in the Fountain #275
Dawn's Gift #303
Brooke's Chance #323
Betting Man #344
Silver Sands #362
Lost and Found #384
Out of the Cold #440
Sophie's Attic #725
Not Just Another Perfect Wife #818
Haven's Call #859

JOAN ELLIOTT PICKART

is the author of over seventy novels. When she isn't writing, she enjoys watching football, knitting, reading, gardening and attending craft shows on the town square. Joan has three all-grown-up daughters and a fantastic little grandson. In September of 1995, Joan traveled to China to adopt her fourth daughter, Autumn. Joan and Autumn have settled into their cozy cottage in a charming small town in the high pine country of Arizona.

Chapter One

The delicate hummingbird hovered in space, flitted away, then returned to dip its long, curved beak into the enticing red syrup in the feeder hanging from the edge of the patio roof.

Moments later the tiny bird was joined by another. They sipped the delicious offering, fluttered in perfect unison once around the plastic feeder, then zoomed off, flying close together.

Janice Jennings smiled in delight as she watched her morning visitors disappear from view. She hadn't moved, had hardly breathed, while the pair of hummingbirds enjoyed their breakfast, not wishing to do anything to frighten them away.

"Have a safe and adventuresome day, my little friends," Janice said softly.

She resumed the soothing task of brushing her freshly shampooed, wavy blond hair that fell to the middle of her back. Closing her eyes, she allowed her senses to take over.

She savored the warmth of the rising sun on her face as it peeked beneath the patio roof.

She could feel the strands of her hair beginning to dry, the waves rippling beneath the bristles of the brush.

The aroma of roses reached her from the blossoming bushes lining one side of the fenced yard, and she caught the faint, pungent scent of chlorine wafting from the sparkling blue water in the swimming pool.

The lingering taste of the cinnamon tea she'd had earlier tempted her to indulge in another cup.

She heard the chirping of happy birds, a dog barking in the distance, then the satisfied meow of a cat.

Janice sighed in contentment and opened her eyes, fluffing her hair with her free hand to be certain it was dry. Setting the brush on the round, glass-topped table next to her, she stretched her arms leisurely above her head, then dropped her hands into her lap.

This was her favorite time of day, she thought, not for the first time. It was definitely worth waking far earlier than was necessary in order to savor the sight of the breathtaking Arizona sunrise, drink her tea and watch the hummingbirds arrive for breakfast. She allowed the tranquility of the early morning to fill her to overflowing before heading off to what would be a busy day.

Janice glanced at the thin, gold watch on her wrist and frowned.

The minutes passed far too quickly during her morning ritual, she thought, getting to her feet.

She slipped the brush into the pocket of her mint-green, satin robe, picked up the china saucer holding the wafer-thin teacup and entered the house through the double doors that led to the backyard.

As she stepped into the large, sunny kitchen, she shifted her thoughts to what needed to be done when she arrived at her boutique, Sleeping Beauty.

A shipment of bath accessories had arrived just before closing time the evening before. The soaps, oils, crystals and powders would have to be unpacked and checked off against the bill.

All the products would need price stickers attached, then some would go in the storage room, the remainder on the waiting shelves in the store.

She also had to mark down the silk and satin teddies for a special sale that would begin tomorrow, plus give thought to a new display for the front window.

"Busy, busy, busy," Janice said aloud as she washed and dried the cup and saucer by rote. She left the kitchen and headed toward the master bedroom.

The sprawling, four-bedroom house that Janice had purchased less than a year ago was a south-western ranch style, white adobe with a white-gravel roof.

The rooms were large and airy, with archways leading to the living room, formal dining room and hallways. The master suite was on one side of the structure; the other three bedrooms, which were still empty of furnishings, were located on the other side.

Janice's toes sank into the plush, pale salmon-colored carpeting as she walked down the hall.

She had decorated with a light hand. The living room bore only a floral-patterned sofa, oak end tables and lamps, a glass-topped, oak coffee table and two easy chairs, one white, the other mint-green and white-striped.

The effect was exactly what she'd strived to achieve. The room was welcoming, though spacious, with no overabundance of furniture to mar the simplistic beauty.

In a whimsical moment she'd added a cluster of woven Native American baskets that were grouped next to the hearth of the flagstone fireplace.

One basket was filled with dried desert flowers; another held potpourri that Janice had made from the petals of the roses in the backyard. A chubby little basket boasted an array of shiny marbles and another creation hugged skeins of varying shades of yarn.

She had yet to find any pictures or other decorations for the walls of the main part of the house. The only framed print that she owned so far was a pastel painting of two hummingbirds hovering over a splash of vibrant roses. It hung in a place of honor above her bed.

For her bedroom, Janice had chosen an oak, king-size bed with a matching dresser and chest of drawers. The bedspread was salmon and mint-green stripes with fluffy shams. A round table had a matching skirt that fell in soft folds to the floor, and an oak slipper rocker was placed next to the table.

A huge walk-in closet covered one entire wall and was fronted by gleaming mirrors.

As Janice crossed the bedroom, her attention was diverted by her reflection in the mirrored wall. She stopped and turned, her gaze sweeping over her image.

The satin robe clung to her full breasts and gently sloping hips. The rich material accentuated long legs and her slender five-foot-eight-inch frame. Her hair was a wild tumble of golden waves.

Janice tilted her head to one side, produced a phony smile that was reflected back at her, then in the next instant crossed her eyes and stuck out her tongue.

Her smile faded as she slid one panel of the closet door open to select what she would wear.

She was beautiful, she thought dryly. And that beauty had brought her nothing but misery for the majority of her twenty-eight years.

"Don't start dwelling on *that*," she muttered. "You'll ruin what has started out to be a lovely day."

Twenty minutes later, Janice left the house.

Her hair was pulled back into a severe figure-eight chignon at the nape of her neck.

She wore a boxy, tan summer suit, the skirt a size too large, the jacket hanging loosely above it.

Sturdy, tan Oxfords were on her feet, and a pair of heavy, black-framed glasses were perched on her nose.

There were no prescription lenses in the glasses, nor was there one speck of makeup on her face.

Janice slid behind the wheel of a no-frills, white compact car and drove away from the house, the image she'd seen reflected in her bedroom mirror forgotten as she headed for Sleeping Beauty.

Taylor Sinclair carried a mug of coffee to the kitchen table and sat down across from his father, Clem.

As Clem executed the morning ritual of giving Scamp, his ten-year-old Irish setter, crusts of toast, Taylor scrutinized his father.

His dad looked old, he thought, frowning. There was a gray pallor to his skin that was disturbing, and an aura of weariness seemed to emanate from him.

"How are you, Dad?" Taylor said. Fine, never better, he answered himself. The question and response were always the same.

"Fine, never better," Clem said. "That's it, Scamp. There's no more toast."

The dog flopped onto the floor and rested his

head on his front paws as he stared up at Clem with sorrowful brown eyes.

"Dramatics won't get you a thing, you old hound," Clem said chuckling, then directed his attention to Taylor. "So! Fill me in. How was your trip up to Prescott?"

"I enjoyed it." Taylor took a sip of the strong, black coffee. "This isn't decaf. I thought the doctor said…"

"I can't stomach that decaf stuff," Clem interrupted, waving one hand dismissively in the air. "A man has to have a decent cup of coffee to get going in the morning." He paused. "Prescott?"

"Okay. We won't discuss your breaking the rules about the coffee," Taylor said, shaking his head in defeat. "The five people who own businesses in Prescott and who dug in their heels and refused to get a new accountant when you left there all send you their best wishes."

Clem smiled and nodded.

"Martha at the café," Taylor went on, "said now that you're retired she doesn't want to hear that you've gotten fat and sassy from sitting on your rump."

"Ah, those Prescott folks are good people. I'd like to see all of them. But because of my bum ticker, the doctor won't allow me to even visit Prescott anymore, let alone make my home there. You wouldn't think that a bit of altitude would have such an impact on a person."

"A mile high isn't a *bit* of altitude, Dad."

Clem sighed. "Yes, I realize that. But even after two years, it's still hard to get accustomed to living in this condo in the Phoenix heat. It's so crowded in this damnable city, too. So fast, busy, and there's so much crime." He paused. "I can remember how your mother and I used to sit on the porch of that grand old house in Prescott where we raised you and talk about where we would travel when I retired."

"Dad..."

"I know, I know. I'm feeling sorry for myself and I should be counting my blessings. It's just that...well, we lost your mother to cancer nearly fifteen years ago now, Taylor, and I seem to miss her more with every passing day. This retirement of mine isn't remotely close to being what I hoped and dreamed it would be."

"You've got to give it a fair chance, Dad," Taylor said, leaning slightly toward him. "It's only been a few weeks.

"I'm encountering a lot of differences here, too, since moving from San Francisco to take over your business. You need to keep an open mind about all the new activities you can try out. How about golf?"

"I've got better things to do than walk my legs off following a silly little white ball over a stretch of lawn that someone painted green."

"Forget golf," Taylor mumbled, then took another sip of coffee.

"What did you think of the job Brandon Hamilton did restoring Hamilton House?" Clem said.

"It's fantastic, really sharp," Taylor said. "Say, you didn't tell me that Brandon got married. I met his wife, Andrea. She's very pleasant, very pretty, and she and Brandon are obviously deeply in love."

"I thought I told you that Brandon got hitched," Clem said, frowning.

"No," Taylor said quietly. "You didn't."

"My memory isn't what it used to be, I guess."

No, it wasn't, Taylor thought glumly. Nor was his father's enthusiasm for life even close to what it once had been.

"Anyway," Taylor began, "Brandon and Andrea are thinking of adding some specialty shops in the lobby of Hamilton House. We sat down and put some numbers together and it's definitely feasible. The hotel is doing very well."

"I know. I did the income tax for that place. Brandon has done a helluva fine job. And now he's married, probably giving thought to having a child." Clem glared at his son. "Unlike some people I could mention."

"Don't start." Taylor chuckled, the deep, rumbly sound an exact echo of his father's laugh. "You know my stand on the issue of marriage. And I'm not alone in wanting to remain a bachelor. Brandon, Ben Rizzoli and I agreed years ago that a single life was the way to go. Brandon obviously forgot the pact we made.

"Me? I had an idyllic childhood in Prescott,

complete with a mother who stayed home and made chocolate-chip cookies from scratch.

"I had parents who were so much in love, they acted like newlyweds every day of their lives."

Taylor shook his head.

"That's my measuring stick for wedded bliss, Dad. What you and Mom had. I've witnessed perfection, and I won't settle for less. In this day and age, what I want just isn't obtainable."

"There's an old-fashioned woman out there somewhere, Taylor," Clem said. "The problem with you is, you're no longer looking for her."

"Got it in one," Taylor said. "I'm a swinging single bachelor and intend to remain one. How's that?"

"It stinks," Clem said. "I want a grandbaby to bounce on my knee."

"Borrow one from a neighbor in this complex. There must be folks in here who have grandchildren who come to visit them."

"Borrow a grandbaby?" Clem said, raising his eyebrows. "Like a library book? That's the dumbest thing I've ever heard."

Taylor shrugged, then drained his mug. "The subject is closed." He set the mug on the table with a thud. "Back to business. I've gone to every client you have here and in Prescott to say hello and introduce myself to those who don't know me.

"You held out one file because you said you needed to talk to me in-depth about that particular client before I made my little social call. Has he at least agreed to my handling his account?''

''It's a she and, yes, she's receptive to your being her accountant with the understanding that the confidentiality she and I had remains firmly in place.''

''That goes without saying. I'd never discuss a client's finances with anyone else.''

''No, no,'' Clem said. ''It encompasses much more than that, Taylor.''

Taylor frowned. ''You're sounding very mysterious. What's the big secret? Who is this woman?''

''Her name is Janice Jennings, and she owns an extremely profitable boutique called Sleeping Beauty. When that old friend of mine retired right after I moved down here to the valley, he recommended me to Janice to be her new accountant.''

Taylor nodded.

''Shortly after that,'' Clem went on, ''Janice expanded her business from just women's sleepwear to include bath accessories and fancy lingerie. Janice is a very savvy businesswoman, seems to have natural instincts as to what will sell to people with money to spare.''

''So far there's nothing unusual about what you're telling me,'' Taylor said.

''I'm getting to it. Don't rush me,'' Clem said, frowning. ''Let's see, where was I? All right, the thing is, Taylor, that Janice insists no one know that she owns Sleeping Beauty.''

''What?'' Taylor said, his eyebrows shooting up.

"That's crazy. Why wouldn't she want to bask in the glory of being highly successful?"

Clem shrugged. "I have no idea. She never confided in me as to her reasoning. She passes herself off as the manager of the store, with a story that the owner lives out of town."

"Weird."

"She's adamant about all this, Taylor. Whenever you're speaking with her in the shop, you must be extremely careful not to say anything that would indicate that she owns the place. I've assured her that you'll comply."

"Are you certain there's nothing illegal going on with this Janice?"

"Positive," Clem said, nodding. "I did her books every month and prepared her income tax return. She's obviously showing every penny of what is a very financially healthy enterprise. She's single with no dependents, apparently has no one to answer to but herself."

"Then why the secrecy?"

"I don't have a clue, but now you can surely understand why I wanted to fill you in on these details before you called on her. The file for Sleeping Beauty is on the coffee table in the living room."

Taylor got to his feet, causing Scamp to raise his head for a moment, then plop it back down on his paws.

"All right," Taylor said. "I'll review the account, then pay Ms. Jennings a visit this afternoon.

That's all I need…an eccentric client. I don't think I'll say thank you for this one, Dad."

"Well, I suppose you could say she's eccentric because of her insistence that she be recognized only as the manager of Sleeping Beauty."

"No joke."

"But Janice is also a very nice, very pleasant young woman. She's attractive, but then again—" Clem shook his head "—she's not."

Taylor laughed. "That statement didn't make one bit of sense."

"No, I suppose it didn't, but you'll understand what I mean once you've met her."

"This is all beginning to sound very intriguing. The thing is, with all the new clients I inherited from you that I've yet to become familiar with as far as their accounts go, I really don't need the hassle of playing cloak and dagger with your Janice Jennings."

"She's *your* Janice Jennings now, son."

"Dandy," Taylor said dryly.

That afternoon the mailman entered Sleeping Beauty and handed Janice a stack of envelopes.

"Thank you, Henry," she said, smiling. "Has that grandbaby of yours arrived yet?"

"Nope," Henry said. "We're all on pins and needles. My daughter is three days overdue now, my wife is a wreck and my son-in-law is coming unglued. My daughter is the only calm one among us."

"Well, keep me posted," Janice said.

"You bet. See you tomorrow."

"'Bye," Janice said, then began to shuffle through the mail.

A glossy, triple-folded, color brochure caught her eye and she set the other envelopes on the counter to examine the advertisement.

"Oh," she said, reading the information.

She was definitely going to mark this event on her calendar, she thought. An artist was having his debut showing at a Scottsdale gallery. Maybe she'd find a picture for one of the walls of her house.

She mentally shrugged. But if she didn't, she didn't. There was no rush to finish decorating the first home she'd ever owned. She was thoroughly enjoying taking her time, purchasing only what were the perfect additions when she found them.

Besides, it wasn't as though she was continually explaining her not-yet-completed projects to guests. The only people to enter her home, other than the men who had delivered the furniture, were her accountant, Clem, and her neighbor and friend, Shirley Henderson.

Friend. Yes, Shirley was her friend, her *only* friend. The other people she knew were acquaintances. She didn't date, so there was no escort-for-the-evening arriving at her door.

Her life, Janice supposed, would appear rather bleak and lonely to someone examining it, but it suited her perfectly. It was just the way she wanted it.

Janice's musings were interrupted by three laughing and chattering women who came into the boutique.

"Good afternoon," Janice said pleasantly. "May I help you with something, or would you prefer to just browse?"

One of the women walked over to the counter.

"We're shopping for gifts for Mindy Winterson's bridal shower. One of our friends said that Mindy was registered here, and that you would be able to tell us what has already been purchased for our little bride-to-be."

"Certainly." Janice reached beneath the counter for an oblong, puffy, white-covered ledger. She set it on the counter and flipped it open. "Winterson." She lifted a tab with a *W* printed on it. "Yes, here she is. I see she's having a June wedding."

The woman laughed. "With the reception inside an air-conditioned country club, thank goodness."

Janice turned the ledger around so the woman could read the neat writing on the lined page.

"Oh, dear," the woman said. "Look at all the goodies Mindy is already receiving. Could you help us find gifts that will be different from the others? This is Mindy's favorite store, and we'd hate to go anywhere else for her presents."

"We'll put together a lovely ensemble for her," Janice said. "There's a great deal left to choose from, and we can coordinate it if we use our imaginations."

"Excellent. Oh, this is going to be such fun."

Janice left the ledger open so the women could refer to it, then slid the mail into a wire basket on the top shelf beneath the counter, not aware that the gallery brochure slipped free and landed next to the cash register. She emerged from behind the counter to assist the women in their shopping spree.

Fifteen minutes later a vast array of items sat next to the ledger, with the women declaring they were far from finished selecting gifts for their darling Mindy.

"We've just added scented candles to the inventory," Janice said. "We have aromas that match the soaps, oils and bath beads."

"Marvelous," one of the women said, then laughed. "I'm going to buy two of whatever I like. I'm due for some delicious pampering myself."

"Aren't we all?" Janice said, smiling. "If you'll follow me, I'll show you what we have."

Outside of Sleeping Beauty, Taylor gave the window display a thorough perusal.

Classy stuff, he thought. The high quality of the feminine garments was evident even through a panel of glass. Nice variety, too. A couple of the whatever-they-were—teddies?—were sexy as hell; another was more sedate. That white satin nightgown with the matching robe would cling to every enticing, feminine curve of a woman's body.

This was *not* a store that a man would feel comfortable in, Taylor thought, frowning. Did guys really march inside to shop for their lady, just as bold as you please?

"Not me," he mumbled. "Not in this lifetime."

Enough stalling, Sinclair, he told himself. Standing on the sidewalk wasn't going to accomplish his mission of introducing himself to the mysterious Janice Jennings.

With a resigned sigh, he strode to the door and entered Sleeping Beauty.

Chapter Two

Janice looked up when she heard the door to the shop open. She did a double take when she saw that the new arrival was a man.

She would rather deal with the most hard-to-please female customer, she thought, frowning, than a member of the male species.

During the five years that Sleeping Beauty had existed, she had yet to have a man come into the boutique who was totally at ease in the femininity-personified environment.

They either fidgeted and mumbled, anxious for the moment when they could make their escape, or they covered their embarrassment with sexual innuendos regarding the offered apparel.

Then there were those who attempted to give the

impression that they shopped for women's lingerie every day of the week. They whipped out charge cards and grabbed hangers off the rack willy-nilly, with no thought to size or color coordination.

Which category would this male customer fall into? Janice wondered. He was certainly good-looking, she'd give him that. He was, in fact, the most ruggedly handsome man to step foot into her frilly domain.

He was tall, at least six feet, and he had thick, light brown hair that was sun-streaked to nearly blond in places. His dark suit, complemented by a crisp white shirt and dark tie, was obviously custom-tailored, accentuating his broad shoulders and long, muscular legs. His features were chiseled enough to keep him from being tagged a pretty boy.

He was the type of man who had to beat women off with a stick, the kind who could pick and choose his companion for an evening from the most beautiful women available in the swinging singles scene.

He could be married, Janice mused, but she seriously doubted it. Experience had taught her that men like this one weren't interested in settling down for a lifetime with one woman.

Why should they, when there was an endless stream of glamorous females willing and able to keep them company and warm their beds?

As he stood, sweeping his gaze over the store, she realized he was not going to disappear simply because she wished he would.

"Would you excuse me a moment?" Janice said

to the women, who were examining the scented candles.

"Yes, certainly," one of them said. "Take your time. These candles are wonderful, and we can select our own bath accessories to go with the ones we like."

"Fine," Janice said, smiling. "I'll get back to you as quickly as I can."

She turned and started toward the man, who was still perched just inside the door.

So here she was, the mysterious Janice Jennings, Taylor thought as he watched the woman approach him. She was tall, and moved with a gracefulness that was either natural, or had been practiced for many years.

Her face was very, *very* pretty, with delicate features, big blue eyes and kiss-me-right-now lips.

But...

What had his father said? Oh, yes, now he remembered. Clem had remarked that Janice Jennings was attractive, but then again she wasn't.

That strange statement hadn't made one bit of sense at the time, but now it did. There was something not quite....*right* about Ms. Jennings.

The woman stopped several feet in front of Taylor and produced a small smile.

"May I help you find a particular item," she said. "Or would you prefer to browse?"

There was *definitely* something wrong here, Taylor thought. Up close, Janice was even more beautiful than she'd appeared from across the room.

Long, dark lashes emphasized sapphire eyes despite the heavy, dark-framed glasses she wore. Her skin was peaches and cream, dewy, absolutely lovely. Her voice had caressed him like plush velvet and caused an instantaneous coil of heat to tighten low in his body.

The sun was cascading directly over her blond hair, turning it into a shiny golden halo that made his fingers tingle with the urge to pull the pins from her matronly bun and allow the tresses to fall free.

As far as he could tell, Janice wore no makeup, not even a touch of lipstick. And that suit she had on? What a horrendous outfit.

His father was right. Janice Jennings was very attractive, but then again…she wasn't. It didn't add up. How could a woman who was highly successful selling extremely feminine apparel be so oblivious to her *own* femininity?

"Sir?"

"What?" Taylor said, jerked back from his rambling thoughts. "Oh. I'm Taylor Sinclair, Ms. Jennings. Your new accountant. I'd like to speak with you, if I may? You're obviously busy and I'm in no rush. I'll just wait until you're free."

"You're Clem's son?" Janice said, her frown deepening. Taylor was single, she remembered, because she'd asked Clem if his son would be moving a family to Phoenix from San Francisco, providing grandchildren to fill some of Clem's retirement hours.

Taylor smiled. "In the flesh."

Good grief, Janice thought, feeling an unwelcome shiver course down her spine. Taylor Sinclair's smile was deadly.

Well, she wasn't *impressed* by the oh-so-masculine and gorgeous Mr. Sinclair. He was the love-'em-and-leave-'em type. She knew how they operated, and she didn't like them one iota.

Taylor Sinclair was the last kind of man she'd choose to do business with.

Janice sighed.

She did *not* want Taylor to be her accountant, but the idea of finding a new one held little appeal. She had been secure in the knowledge that Clem would never divulge that she was the owner of Sleeping Beauty. Clem had been adamant that his son would be equally discreet.

Well, so be it. It was the "bird in the hand" theory. Her secret was safe with a Sinclair, and the peace of mind that brought her was worth a great deal. She didn't have to like Taylor to be his client, and it wasn't as though she'd have that much contact with him, anyway.

"All right," Janice said, nodding. "If you don't mind waiting until I'm free, that's fine with me. Make yourself at home, Mr. Sinclair."

"It's Taylor...Janice," he said, producing another hundred-watt smile. "I like to be on a first-name basis with my clients. I realize that you're the manager of Sleeping Beauty and not the owner, but my father explained that I would be dealing directly with you.''

"That's correct," she said, lifting her chin. "The owner lives out of state."

"Mmm," he said.

"Yes...mmm."

Janice narrowed her eyes, then spun around on her clunky shoes to rejoin the women who were still examining the bath products.

Taylor watched her go, noting the perfection of her shapely calves and delicate ankles. But her feet sported a somebody's-grandmother style of shoes.

Yes, indeed, he thought, Ms. Sleeping Beauty was a mysterious woman, a puzzle to be solved. There were so many questions surrounding the enigmatic Janice.

And finding the answers could prove to be challenging and very, *very* interesting.

Curbing a smile, Taylor began to wander aimlessly around the store, at times nodding in approval at the manner in which Janice had displayed the merchandise.

Mounted on the many racks of hanger-held apparel were gleaming, oval glass stands where color-coordinated items were displayed. Janice had added extra touches to the array that made it far from the ordinary.

There was a single, white silk rose nestled on a satin scarf; another display had a silver framed photograph of a bride and groom, while yet another had sparkling crystal perfume bottles.

The lady was good at this, Taylor thought. She knew how to make things ultra-classy, and the price tags he'd taken a peek at said she assumed that her customers were prepared to pay for the extra oomph.

Yes, his father had been right when he'd said that Janice was a savvy businesswoman, and the file on Sleeping Beauty that he'd studied before coming here also verified that fact.

The only thing off-kilter was Janice herself. Didn't she look in the mirror when she got dressed in the morning? Couldn't she see the beautiful swan beneath the ugly duckling duds she decked herself out in?

Beautiful swan? his mind echoed. He was getting poetic in his thirty-sixth year, and more than a tad corny. But, cripe, the way Janice presented herself didn't make any sense.

Was she totally oblivious to her womanly attributes? Or...now there was an intriguing thought...was Janice *purposely* diminishing her beauty? If that was the case, then why? What was she afraid of? What was she hiding from?

Taylor stopped at the counter, then leaned back against it, crossing one ankle over the other as he settled in to wait for Janice. His glance fell on a color brochure and he picked it up absently.

Say now, he thought, reading the advertisement, this was right up his alley. He was always eager to see the work of a new artist with the hope of adding another piece of artwork to his growing collection.

He made a mental note of the day, time and place of the exhibit, then put the brochure back on the counter.

And waited.

"That man is so handsome, he's enough to make a woman weep," one of the women said to Janice. "Is he yours?"

"Mine?" Janice said, her eyes widening. "Heavens, no. He's the accountant."

"He doesn't fit the image of an accountant," the woman said, then laughed. "I can think of lots of things to do with a hunk like that one instead of balancing the books."

"Ditto," one of the other women said. "Is he married?"

"No," Janice said. "Have you selected the candles and bath accessories you prefer?"

"Not married." The woman sighed wistfully. "There was a time when men like that gave me second looks, but that was ten years and twenty pounds ago."

"You have a lovely figure," Janice said. "If you lost twenty pounds, you'd be much too thin."

"You know the old saying," the woman said, smiling. "You can't be too rich or too thin."

"Our society places far too much emphasis on outward appearances," Janice said, frowning.

"Maybe so," the woman said, shrugging. "But

facts are facts, and they're not going to change. Take our bride-to-be Mindy, for example. She never dated, never had a boyfriend. Then? She lost fifty pounds, learned how to apply makeup to her best advantage, and had her hair styled to flatter her face. Bingo. She's getting married.''

"Exactly," the other woman said. "Mindy would still be lonely and miserable if she hadn't made the changes in her appearance that she did."

"But that's wrong, don't you see?" Janice said.

"No, dear," the woman said. "That's life."

What on earth was she doing? Janice thought. She was getting into a debate with customers, for heaven's sake, climbing up on her soapbox.

And it was all Taylor Sinclair's fault.

This whole topic of conversation had gotten started because Taylor was in the store, hanging around as though he owned the place.

He should have telephoned for an appointment instead of just dropping in. Whatever mundane thing he wanted to talk to her about could have waited until after the store was closed for the day.

Janice slid a glance at Taylor where he was propped against the counter.

Look at him, she fumed. He was so relaxed, so obviously comfortable in the midst of women's lingerie, he appeared as though he might nod off. He'd probably seen so much feminine finery being removed in his bedroom that it was no big deal to be surrounded by it.

Why did Clem Sinclair have a son like Taylor?

She was well and truly stuck with him, because she had no desire to find another accountant whom she could thoroughly trust.

So, okay, fine. She'd conduct her financial affairs with Taylor, but that sure as heck didn't mean that she had to like him. Not even close.

"Well, I believe we're finally set," one of the women said, bringing Janice back to attention. "Get your charge cards out, my friends. It's time to pay up for our shopping spree."

Taylor moved out of the way as the group approached the counter. He watched from a distance, noting the efficient manner in which Janice rang up the sales, tended to the charge cards, then began to pack the multitude of items the women had purchased.

There were the classy touches again, he thought. The tissue paper Janice used was pale pink. The boxes and the bags with twine handles were one shade darker, all bearing the name of the store in embossed letters in the same flowing script as the sign outside.

Yes, indeed, Janice Jennings knew her stuff, and the profit figures he'd studied in the file were proof of that puddin'.

The women collected their packages, thanked Janice for her wonderful assistance and left the store, managing to direct smiles at Taylor as they went. He smiled and nodded at them politely as they exited, then a sudden silence fell over the boutique.

Taylor looked at Janice for a long moment, then started slowly toward the counter.

Dear heaven, Janice thought as another shiver coursed through her. Taylor Sinclair moved with a lazy grace that reminded her of a sleek cat advancing on its prey. And at the moment, that prey was her!

Get a grip, she admonished herself. The man was an accountant, not a panther, or whatever. She was being ridiculous.

She tugged on the hem of her jacket, lifted her chin and met Taylor's gaze directly when he stopped in front of her on the other side of the counter.

"Now then, Mr. Sinclair," she said, her voice not quite steady, "just what is it that I can do for you?"

For starters, Taylor thought, she could allow him to pull the pins from her hair, freeing that golden halo from the matronly bun she wore it in to discover how long her silky, blond hair was.

Taylor cleared his throat as a coil of heat tightened low in his body.

"It's Taylor, remember?" he said.

"Yes, fine," Janice said with an exasperated little sigh. "What do you want...Taylor?"

What a question to ask, he thought as heat rocketed through him. Hell, this was crazy. Why on earth would a woman who looked as if she was playing dress-up in her grandmother's clothes be capable of pushing his libido buttons?

To say that Janice Jennings wasn't his type was putting it very mildly. He dated women who knew they were beautiful and enjoyed every minute of it.

If he mentally placed those women on the North Pole, Janice would be so removed from them he'd have to invent a location farther away than the South Pole.

Granted, Janice had incredible eyes behind those heavy-framed glasses. And her face was lovely, really exquisite, her skin reminding him of a fresh peach. And the length of her legs visible to his perusal were shapely and—damn it, Sinclair. This was insane.

"Taylor?" Janice said, frowning. "Are you asleep with your eyes open?"

"What?" he said. "Oh, I'm sorry. I was thinking about something." He cleared his throat and ran one hand down his tie. "I've reviewed your file, Janice, and I'd like to sit down with you and discuss it."

"Why?" she said, still frowning. She glanced around quickly to be certain no one was in the store. "What could there possibly be to discuss? I assume that all the information about Sleeping Beauty was in that file, clear as a bell...my profit and loss, the number of employees I have, how much I pay in income taxes, and on and on."

"Taxes," Taylor said. "You're paying far more than is necessary."

Janice's eyes widened slightly. "Are you insinuating that your father miscalculated my tax figures?''

"No, no, of course not," he said quickly, raising both hands. "My father is...*was* a top-notch accountant." He dragged a hand through his hair.

My, my, Janice thought. Taylor's hair was so thick and styled so perfectly that it fell right back into place after his long fingers burrowed through it. He really did have very nice hair. Oh, for Pete's sake, why was she wasting her mental energies thinking about Taylor's hair?

"My taxes?" she said, raising her eyebrows.

"Yes. My dad did an excellent job for you. The thing is, I'm a bit more aggressive, shall we say, than my father."

The sudden image of dear, sweet Clem swooping down on the female populace with a knock-'em-dead smile and a sexier-than-all-get-out way of walking like his son struck Janice as hysterically funny.

And so she laughed.

"A bit more aggressive?" she managed to say. "That's a tad understated." She continued to laugh, shaking her head.

Lord, Taylor thought, listen to that musical sound. And Janice's eyes were sparkling, actually sparkling, like blue diamonds. Her smile lit up that beautiful face and her lips... Man, those lips were begging to be kissed.

The heat, that damnable heat, low in his body

was pulsing, tightening to the point of pain. Enough of this nonsense.

"Are you finished?" he said, glaring at Janice.

"I think so," she said, then drew a wobbly breath. "Oh, my, that was funny." She paused. "There. Yes, I'm fine now."

"I missed the joke," Taylor said dryly. "Would you care to explain what set you off?"

"No," she said, another bubble of laughter escaping. "Just forget it. You have my full attention."

"Yes, well, as I said, I'd like to sit down and discuss Sleeping Beauty with you, including what might be feasible for the future."

"The future?" she said thoughtfully, cocking her head slightly to one side. "I've done all that I can at this location. I took over the place next door and doubled my square footage. By signing a five-year lease, I was able to get the owner of the complex to punch a hole through the adjoining wall, meeting my design specifications."

"And the lease holds him to the same rent for five years," Taylor said, nodding, "which was very smart on your part."

"Thank you," she said, smiling. "I was rather pleased with myself about that negotiation."

Janice, please don't smile, Taylor begged silently. Not right now. Not when the coiled heat low in his body was driving him up the wall.

"So," Janice said, shrugging. "The future of the

boutique is set. I've added the bath accessories and they're selling extremely well.

"The woman of today is more self-assured than ever before. She knows her own worth and pampers herself when she feels the need. She doesn't rely on others to validate her existence. She does it herself. Sleeping Beauty is reaping the rewards of the modern woman's mind-set."

"That sounded like an outtake from a speech."

"It was," she said, laughing. "I was the speaker at a Women in Business meeting last month. That was part of my spiel."

And don't laugh, either, Taylor thought. Damn it, this woman was tying him up in knots, which was so asinine it was a crime.

"Therefore," Janice said breezily, "we have nothing to discuss regarding the future of Sleeping Beauty."

"Wrong," Taylor said. "Your profits are such that you're paying exorbitant taxes. There are ways to solve that problem." He paused. "I'd like to suggest that we have a business dinner, talk things over in a relaxed atmosphere while enjoying a good meal."

"Oh, I don't think—"

"My father and I have both found that a pleasant environment is much more conducive to fresh ideas and open minds than an appointment in an office. It's true. Trust me."

Trust Taylor Sinclair? Janice thought incredulously. Oh, ha. Not a chance. Trust Mr. Dynamite

Smile, Nonstop Body and Practiced Charisma? No way.

Oh, wait a minute. She was off and running on the wrong track. Taylor wasn't viewing her as a woman. He saw her as nothing more than a client. The hours they would spend together would be strictly business.

Trust him? Yes, she would, because she had total confidence in Clem, and knew the dear man had seen to it that she was in expert financial hands.

"Tomorrow night?" Taylor said. "Seven o'clock? I have your address on file, so I'll pick you up."

"That's not necessary. Why don't we just meet at a restaurant?" Janice said.

"My father would skin me alive," Taylor said, smiling. "He made it a practice to pick up and deliver clients for lunch and dinner meetings. He'd expect me to do the same, especially for someone I've inherited from him."

"Well, I just think it would be simpler if I met you at—"

The door to the shop abruptly opened and two women entered.

"Hello, hello, Janice," one of the women said. "Did the scented candles arrive yet?"

"They certainly did," Janice said, smiling. "And they're lovely."

"Wonderful," the woman said. "Betty and I are here to splurge."

"I'm gone," Taylor said, rapping his knuckles

on the counter. "Tomorrow night, Janice. I'll pick you up at seven."

"But…"

"It was a pleasure to meet you, Ms. Jennings," he said, then turned and strode toward the door. "Ladies," he said, smiling at the two women as he passed them.

"But…" Janice said again, then sighed.

So much for meeting Taylor at a restaurant. Tomorrow night the first eligible gentleman caller would step over the threshold of her safe haven.

Well, no, not really. Taylor wasn't a man, he was an accountant. If the meeting would benefit Sleeping Beauty, then so be it. The boutique was her raison d'être, the focal point of her entire existence.

So, yes, she'd go out to dinner with Taylor Sinclair and simply pretend he was Clem with different packaging.

No problem.

Janice frowned.

Then why had a flock of butterflies suddenly taken up residence in her stomach as she thought about tomorrow night at seven o'clock?

Chapter Three

Taylor sat in the high-backed, soft leather chair behind the desk in his office, his legs crossed at the ankle on the edge of the corner of the desk.

He'd removed his jacket and tie, and undone the two top buttons of his shirt. His hands were linked behind his head as he cradled the telephone receiver between his ear and shoulder.

"And there you have it, Brandon," he said into the receiver. "I truly believe Sleeping Beauty is an excellent candidate for one of the specialty shops you're planning to put in the lobby of Hamilton House."

"Sounds promising," Brandon said. "I'll talk to Andrea about it. Do you think Janice Jennings would be interested in a small outlet up here in Prescott?"

"No telling. I wasn't in a position to discuss it with her today. Besides, I wouldn't have broached the subject with her until I'd spoken with you. I'm having a business dinner with Janice tomorrow night so I could bring it up then, if I get a go-ahead from you."

"All right," Brandon said. "I'll be back to you sometime tomorrow. We want top-of-the-line for those shops. One hundred percent classy."

"The merchandise Janice carries in her boutique would give you that…big time," Taylor said. "It's expensive as hell, too, but the women I saw in there today didn't blink an eye at the prices." He paused. "Where do you stand with the architect who's drawing up the plans for the shops?"

"He's bringing some ideas over here tonight for Andrea and me to look at. We gave him the money figures we worked out with you, and he said he was certain we'd get the effect we want with what he has to play with. We're moving forward very quickly on this, Taylor, because we'd like the shops up and running before we miss out entirely on the summer visitors."

"Good thinking."

"Hamilton House is booked solid through the summer already, and those folksies have money to spend. So far we have a local florist who is very interested in coming into one of the shops. Andrea is also talking to a representative from a megabucks candy outfit."

"I'm impressed," Taylor said. "You're hustling, Hamilton."

"You bet we are. Listen, when you're talking to Janice, remember to tell her that even though she may have an advertising contract for her Phoenix store, the shops in Hamilton House become the clients of Andrea's advertising firm."

"Got it. I must say that you and Andrea are a good team."

"In more ways than one. I'm telling you, Taylor, Andrea is the best thing that ever happened to me. Lord, I love that woman. I didn't realize how empty my existence was until she came along. You'd do well to take a close look at *your* life-style, old buddy."

Taylor laughed. "You sound like my father. He wants a grandbaby to bounce on his knee. I told him to take up golf, which got my head handed to me. I'm delighted that you're a happily married man, Brandon, but I'll pass. I don't want any part of that scene."

"That's what *I* thought," Brandon said, "until I fell in love with Andrea. Humor me, okay? Project how you're living now into the far future. There's nothing comforting about the picture of growing old alone. Hell, man, you could be lonely even as we speak and not even know it. That sure was true about me. Will you think about what I'm saying?"

"Yeah, yeah, sure. I'll pencil it in on my calendar. I'll schedule a 'getting in touch with my inner self,' or whatever."

"You're dusting me off, Sinclair," Brandon said.

"In spades, Hamilton. Marriage isn't right for everyone, Brandon. I know who I am, and the hearth and home, wife and babies number is not where I'm at. Never has been. Never will be."

"We'll see."

"Enough of this. Call me tomorrow after you've discussed Janice and Sleeping Beauty with Andrea."

"Yep. Talk to you then. Say hello to your father for me. See ya, Taylor."

"'Bye."

Taylor dropped his feet to the floor, then leaned forward to replace the receiver. He stood and walked to the windows that made up one wall of the office, shoving his hands into his pockets as he stared out over the skyline of Phoenix.

Well, he'd started the ball rolling.

If Brandon and Andrea told him to present the Hamilton House idea to Janice, would she be receptive to the proposed plan? He didn't have a clue.

In fact, he didn't have a clue about a lot of things regarding Ms. Jennings. But one thing was for certain. The dinner meeting with her tomorrow night wouldn't be boring. Depending on Brandon and Andrea's decision, he and Janice just might have a great deal to discuss.

Taylor shook his head. Brandon was worse than someone who had quit smoking and felt driven to save the world's smokers from their nasty habit. Hamilton was happily married and, therefore, his bachelor friends should run right out and find themselves wives.

"Sorry, buddy," Taylor said aloud. "Not interested."

You could be lonely even as we speak and not even know it.

Taylor frowned as Brandon's words echoed loudly in his mind.

He was *not* lonely. Yeah, sure, he was new in town, had just moved to Phoenix from San Francisco, but he already knew an amazing number of people from past business dealings.

He'd met a couple of his neighbors in the apartment building where he now lived, and he was going to play tennis with one of the clients he'd inherited from his father.

And women? They'd come along soon enough. They always did. A city the size of Phoenix wouldn't be lacking in the beautiful, no-commitments gals who made up his social life.

A sudden image of Janice flitted in Taylor's mental vision and his frown deepened.

Where had *she* come from out of the blue? Thinking about the women he would no doubt begin dating in the very near future certainly shouldn't have conjured up Janice in his mind's eye.

Granted, Janice Jennings had the most incredibly beautiful, sapphire-colored eyes that he had ever seen.

And, yes, her lips made him want to pull her into his arms and claim her mouth with his.

And, okay, Janice had, for some unexplainable and annoying reason, caused heated desire to rocket through him.

But Janice wasn't his type, not even close. Her mode of dress announced that she wasn't a sophisticated woman.

She was…she was frumpy, for crying out loud. She was—

Forget it, Taylor told himself. He'd wasted enough mental energy already, contemplating why Janice made no attempt to heighten her natural, womanly attributes.

So what if she wasn't aware of her beauty?

So what if she knew but didn't care?

So what if she was *intentionally* diminishing it, hiding it for heaven only knew what reason?

His curiosity was aroused by the mysterious Ms. Jennings. Not only was her wardrobe an interesting puzzle, but so was her demand that her ownership of Sleeping Beauty be kept a deep, dark secret.

If he discovered the answers to his questions about Janice, hooray for him. If he didn't, it was no big deal. She was just another client, nothing more. He had no time to dwell on the off-the-wall Ms. Jennings.

You could be lonely even as we speak and not even know it.

Brandon's words hammered once again in Taylor's mind.

"Damn it, Hamilton," he muttered. "Quit playing with my head. You're so off base it's a crime."

A passing cloud covered the brilliant sun, casting a shadow over the office. A strange chill swept through Taylor and he spun around, his eyes darting back and forth across the large room.

He'd felt...something, he thought. It was as though... Lord, how weird...as though an invisible hand had tapped him on the shoulder to gain his attention.

Hell, this was crazy. There was nothing here but an expensively furnished office. He'd hung his framed diplomas on the wall to replace the ones his father had removed. Other than that, everything was exactly the same as when Clem Sinclair had run this lucrative business.

Except...

What?

Taylor dragged both hands down his face.

He was losing it. This was nuts. There was nothing unusual about this room. It suited his tastes close enough that he'd decided to leave it as it was. It remained as it had always been.

Except...

As though drawn by an uncontrollable force, Taylor's gaze was pulled to the large desk, where several files were waiting for his attention.

The chill returned, causing him to shiver.

He walked to the chair and sank onto it heavily, his eyes riveted on the bare, left corner of the desk.

The picture, his mind thundered. The framed

photograph of his parents and him from the night he'd graduated from Prescott High School was no longer there. The family portrait that Clem had enjoyed looking at each day as he worked at that desk was gone. His father had taken it home.

But Taylor had nothing to replace it with.

He didn't have a family.

A wife.

A son.

Damn it, he thought, lunging to his feet. What was the matter with him? He didn't *want* the lifestyle his father had had.

Clem had loved his wife, Margaret—more, it seemed, with every passing day. And he'd loved his son with that same all-consuming devotion.

And what had that love and devotion gotten Clem Sinclair in the end? An empty, lonely existence, and an aching heart for what he'd had…and lost. Margaret had died. Taylor was grown, out on his own.

Love was great while it lasted, Taylor thought, dragging one hand through his hair, but there was no guarantee that it would. It was too risky to lay it all on the line.

No way. He wasn't setting himself up to be emotionally defenseless against loneliness and despair. If he never fell in love, then his very soul couldn't be ripped to shreds when it ended.

The spiel he'd given his father that morning about wanting a relationship that mirrored his parents' marriage had been a smoke screen, something to say to hopefully keep his dad from nagging on the subject.

It was also a quiet way of letting his father know that his son respected and admired what his parents had shared.

But there was no escaping the fact that the senior Sinclairs's love, their blissful life together, had ended far earlier than they had hoped.

His secret fears about love were too raw, too personal, to share even with his own father.

Taylor picked up the expensive pen set that had been his parting gift from the powers-that-be at the large company in San Francisco, and slammed it onto the desk where his father's picture frame had rested.

He used such force that the gleaming wooden base holding the pens cracked, causing a jagged white line to mar its perfection.

"Hell," he said.

He'd been working too hard. That was it. He'd put in twelve and eighteen hour days since arriving in Phoenix, paying visits to clients and studying every detail of their files.

He was thinking crazy thoughts, traveling down bizarre mental roads due to being exhausted. He would never change his mind on the risks of loving, never waver from his vow to stay far away from emotional entanglements. For Pete's sake, to have been shaken by the empty corner of a desk was beyond ridiculous.

You could be lonely even as we speak and not even know it.

"That cooks it," Taylor said, a muscle ticking in his jaw.

He strode across the room, yanked open the door to a narrow closet and grabbed his jacket. He left the office, not breaking stride as he passed the desk where the forty-something secretary who had worked for his father looked up at him in surprise.

"I'm outta here," Taylor said gruffly. "I'll be back in the morning, Emily."

"Yes, sir," she said, but Taylor had already disappeared from view. "Goodness," she added, shaking her head in confusion. "What came over *him?*"

That night, for the first time in several years, Janice had the dream.

There had been a time when it had plagued her almost constantly, but then it had ebbed, finally leaving her alone to sleep peacefully.

But tonight it was back.

She was a little girl standing by the front window in a small, shabby apartment, hands flattened on the glass.

"Please, Mama," she said. *"They're playing hopscotch out front. Can I play, too? Please, Mama?"*

"No, absolutely not. What if you fell and scraped your knee, or chin, or elbow? How would that look to the judges of the beauty pageant? Get over here and practice singing your song again."

"I know my song. I want to play hopscotch. I never get to play with my friends."

"They are ordinary children, Janice Jennings, and you are not. You're beautiful, and that's far more important than silly sidewalk games. Your beauty is the only thing that matters. Do you understand me? Your looks are your ticket to a fabulous life, and I intend to see that you get what you deserve. Come away from that window. The sun is too bright there, and I won't have your face marred by freckles."

"But, Mama..." Tears streaming down her cheeks, a sob choked off her plea.

"Quit whining and crying like a baby. You're six years old and you've been taking part in these pageants for three years now. Don't act as though you don't know the rules. Beauty, Janice, that's what counts in this world."

"I don't want to be beautiful. I hate it. I hate it. I—"

Janice sat bolt upright in bed, her heart beating so wildly she could hear the echo of the thundering tempo in her ears.

"I hate it," she whispered.

She pulled her knees up and wrapped her arms around them, resting her moist forehead on top. Her tousled hair fell like a heavy curtain around her face.

"Oh, God," she said, then took a shuddering breath.

She raised her head and swept her hair back with

jerky motions, dashing away the tears that had spilled onto her cheeks.

Why, why, why had the haunting dream returned, evoking the painful memories? Her existence was peaceful, serene, exactly the way she wanted it to be. She'd done nothing different, hadn't changed her pleasant, daily routine.

Except for...

"Dear heaven."

Janice sank back onto the pillow and stared up into the darkness.

Except for accepting Taylor Sinclair's invitation to go out to dinner.

Damn that man. This was all his fault. Taylor was the reason the horrifying dream had returned after such a blessedly long time.

No, no, that wasn't fair. Taylor was simply doing his job. He was getting to know the clients he'd inherited from Clem.

Taylor obviously took his career seriously, just as she did, as evidenced by the fact that he'd thoroughly studied her financial portfolio and was prepared to make suggestions to improve her status even more.

So he was taking the owner of Sleeping Beauty out for a meal, where the conversation would be centered on business. It was an accountant and client outing. *Not* a man and woman on a dinner date.

But she had to admit that Taylor had an unsettling effect on her as a woman. His blatant masculinity had stirred her slumbering femininity, causing shivers of awareness to course through her.

Sleeping Beauty, Janice's mind echoed. The name of her boutique was so perfect. No one knew that it represented her as well as the exquisite apparel she sold. It spoke of her fierce determination to diminish her beauty, to refuse to allow anything, or anyone, to awaken it from it's hidden recesses, never to surface in public again.

Janice sighed with a sense of relief.

She now knew the reason for the dream. The rest was up to her. She would be on full alert against Taylor's masculine magnetism. He was dangerous, a threat to her peace of mind and the life she'd so carefully constructed for herself.

She could handle this. She'd simply be certain that the protective walls she'd built around herself were higher and stronger while she was in close proximity to Taylor.

She was no longer the crying child who ached to play hopscotch.

She was no longer at the mercy of a mother who had only seen the outward beauty of her child, never the lonely and needy inner heart and soul.

Her mother was dead, and so was the man who had married Janice so he could show her off like a beautiful trophy. A man who had betrayed her so painfully.

She was no longer on display to be judged by strangers, who would determine whether or not she was beautiful enough to be accepted.

She was Janice Jennings, in charge, in control, of her own life.

She was Sleeping Beauty.

"Yes," Janice whispered. "Yes."

She closed her eyes and allowed blissful slumber to claim her, no longer afraid of that dream lurking in the shadows.

That afternoon, during a lull at Sleeping Beauty, Janice telephoned one of the women who worked for her and asked if she would be available to take over the store at about two o'clock.

"Sure, Janice," Betsy said. "I'll be happy to come in. I'm getting hooked on television talk shows that are an insult to my gray matter. Even my cat leaves the room when I tune into one of those things."

"Then I'm your heroine," Janice said, laughing. "I'm saving you from yourself."

"That's the truth." Betsy paused. "You're not ill, are you? I can't remember you ever asking me to work when I wasn't scheduled to."

"No, no, I'm fine," she said. "I have a business meeting with the accountant this evening, that's all. I decided to treat myself to the afternoon off, since I'll literally be on duty tonight."

"Good for you," Betsy said. "I suppose you'll have to talk to the owner of Sleeping Beauty and relay every little detail that the accountant said."

"Yes," Janice said slowly. "The owner will be fully informed about what took place."

"Which should earn you another afternoon off. Tell the owner that, Janice."

"I just might. Thanks for stepping in on such short notice. I'll see you in a bit."

"Okeydoke. 'Bye."

"Goodbye, Betsy."

Janice replaced the receiver and smiled.

"Did you get all that, madam owner of Sleeping Beauty?" she said aloud. "I deserve another afternoon free in addition to this one."

Her smile faded and she sighed.

Even after all these years, she wasn't completely comfortable pretending she was only the manager of Sleeping Beauty. But the duplicity was necessary.

"So be it," she said.

She dismissed the subject from her mind as the door to the boutique opened and Henry, the mailman, entered and hurried to the counter.

"It's a girl," he said, beaming as he handed Janice the mail. "Six pounds, six ounces. My daughter is fine. My son-in-law is exhausted. My wife hasn't stopped sniffling with joy, and I'm a proud grandpa."

"Congratulations," Janice said, smiling. "A baby girl. That's wonderful, and how very lucky she is. She's obviously going to be very loved."

"And spoiled," Henry said. "I get to do that, you know. It's in my job description as a grandfather."

Janice laughed. "Indeed, it is." She sobered.

"Remember to give her lots of hugs, Henry, and love her just as she is, no matter what."

"Well, sure, that goes without saying."

"Not always." Janice smiled again. "Anyway, best wishes to you all."

"Thanks, Janice. I gotta go."

Janice watched as Henry left the store, then frowned as flashes from her dream the night before flitted across her mental vision.

"Just love her as she is, Henry, no matter what," she said softly, staring into space. "And give her lots and lots of hugs. And, Henry? Let her play hopscotch whenever she wants to."

Chapter Four

As Janice turned onto her driveway and pressed the button on the remote control to open the garage door, her friend and neighbor, Shirley Henderson, pulled to a stop at the end of the driveway.

"Hello, Janice," Shirley called. "Are you playing hooky this afternoon?"

Janice leaned out the car window. "Well, sort of," she shouted. "Would you like to come over for a swim?"

"You're on. See you in a few."

Janice waved, then drove into the garage, closing the door behind her. She entered the house through the laundry room off the kitchen and headed for her bedroom, removing the pins from her hair as she went.

Shirley was a delight, she thought as she entered the bedroom, shaking her hair free to tumble down her back. She was a rare find as a friend, because she never pried, never pushed for answers to questions that Janice knew she must have.

Shirley often saw her in her work attire, then witnessed the transformation to "Janice at home". But Shirley had never once inquired why there were obviously two Janice Jennings.

"A special friend, indeed," she said aloud as she shed her clothes.

A short time later, Janice stepped out of the kitchen onto the back patio, carrying a tray with tumblers filled with ice and a pitcher of sun tea. She set the refreshments on the table just as Shirley opened the gate to the yard, clad in a one-piece bathing suit and toting a beach towel.

Shirley was forty-three, divorced, and a tad plump. Due to the financial settlement she'd received from a now ex-husband she'd caught in bed with his secretary, she was a woman of leisure who used her spare time to volunteer for several charitable organizations.

Janice enjoyed Shirley's upbeat and cheerful personality. She had told Janice early on that she refused to turn into a bitter old woman due to her husband's betrayal, a decree that Janice had silently vowed to follow.

"Let the bubblehead pick up his dirty socks from now on," she'd said. "Wait until sweetie-poo finds out the bum snores loud enough to rattle the windows. That'll fix her wagon."

Janice had laughed, then said that Shirley's attitude was as refreshing as a spring breeze.

"Hello, Shirley," Janice said, smiling.

"Hi, kiddo," she said, sitting in one of the chairs at the table. "How does a person *sort of* play hooky?"

Janice settled onto the other chair and poured tea into the glasses as she explained that she had a business dinner with her accountant.

"That's my *sort of* playing hooky from the store," Janice said. "I have to go back on duty at seven o'clock."

"Makes sense to me," Shirley said, nodding. "Accountant. I met him, right? I was here when he came one evening to drop off some papers for you. You had just arrived home from work and I followed you in the door with some muffins I'd made. Nice man, grandfatherly type? What was his name? Clem. Yes, that was it. Clem Sinclair."

Janice frowned as she began to twist her hair into a single braid.

"Well, actually," she said, "Clem retired recently. His son, Taylor, has taken over the business. It's Taylor who I'm meeting with tonight."

"Ugh." Shirley wrinkled her nose. "I remember when my attorney passed the baton to his son. The kid was a pompous know-it-all. I switched to another lawyer so fast I left junior still yapping about how wonderful he was. Have you met this Taylor guy yet?''

Janice nodded and wrapped a rubber band around the end of the braid. ''He came into the boutique yesterday.''

''And?'' Shirley raised her eyebrows and took a sip of tea.

Janice delayed answering by swallowing some of her drink.

And? she mentally repeated. Well, Shirley, Taylor Sinclair is without a doubt one of the most ruggedly handsome, *dangerous* men walking this earth.

''He seemed pleasant enough,'' Janice said with a little shrug. ''He feels I'm paying too much income tax and wants to discuss ways to correct that.''

''How boring,'' Shirley said with an unladylike snort of disgust. ''Well, order the most expensive item on the menu. If you have to talk about something as dull as income taxes, at least get a yummy dinner out of the deal.''

''Sounds reasonable to me,'' Janice said, laughing. ''Ready for a swim?''

''Oh, sure. I'll do my doggy paddle bit.''

Janice got to her feet.

''That teeny bikini is the exact color of your eyes,'' Shirley said.

''I know,'' Janice said, glancing down at the skimpy bathing suit. ''I just couldn't resist it. How's that for vain?''

''Yep, that's you. Ms. I've-got-it-so-I-flaunt-it,''

Shirley said, rising. "I'd do that, too, but I have a lot more pounds than I should be flaunting. The thing is, I really don't give a damn."

"Good for you," Janice said, nodding decisively. "Besides, the only witnesses to our flaunting are each other and my darling hummingbirds."

Shortly after six-thirty that evening, Janice stood in front of the wall of mirrors in her bedroom and checked her appearance.

She'd shampooed her hair and reinstated the severe bun at the nape of her neck. Her glasses were once again perched on her nose.

The pale gray suit she wore was a size-too-big duplicate of the one Taylor had seen her in, paired with a high-necked white blouse. The sturdy Oxfords on her feet were a shade darker gray.

Janice smoothed the lapels of the suit jacket and nodded in approval.

Yes, this was the outer appearance she wished to present to the world at large. Excellent.

She turned and crossed the room to sit on the edge of the bed to switch her belongings into a gray leather purse.

But the inner woman? she mused, a small smile touching her lips. Well, that was an entirely different story. Beneath the boxy gray suit she wore peach satin.

Her camisole and the built-in bra were mere whispers of delicate lace, barely covering her full breasts.

The tap pants stroked her skin with satiny smoothness, making her acutely aware of her body, her femininity.

Which was how it should be.

She rejoiced in her womanliness *on her terms*. If a genie suddenly appeared before her and offered to grant her three wishes, she wouldn't even consider using one to be transformed into a man.

No, she liked being a woman. She liked being Janice Jennings, with all that she had accomplished since escaping the manipulation of her mother and husband.

Three wishes from a genie? What a fun and whimsical game to play in her mind. One. Two. Three. What should she wish for? The magical genie was waiting patiently for her first request.

"Chill, genie," she said, getting to her feet with the gray purse in tow. "I have to give this some serious thought. Get comfy, because this could take a while."

She left the bedroom and started down the hall, realizing that her lighthearted mood was diminishing with each step she took in her clunky shoes.

By the time she entered the living room, Janice was frowning.

She did not want to go out to dinner with Taylor Sinclair, she thought, sinking onto the sofa. The evening ahead held no appeal whatsoever.

Butterflies. Those damnable butterflies were back, swooshing around in her stomach like an army intent on jangling her nerves to the maximum.

Being with Taylor was going to result in total exhaustion. She would have to be on full alert every second against the unwelcome and startling effect the man had on her.

Dangerous Taylor Sinclair.

Somehow, she had to mentally paint the word "accountant" in big letters on Taylor's forehead, thinking of him only in those terms.

Janice got to her feet and began to pace around the large room.

She could handle this. She would be fine. What was throwing her for a loop was the fact that she was out of practice, hadn't allowed herself to react to a man since she'd been a freshman in college.

What a disaster that had been. She'd made so many mistakes, born of naiveté due to being on her own for the first time in her life, due to the deaths of her mother and husband.

She'd burst onto the Arizona State University campus with excitement she could barely contain, her entire future spread before her like a banquet of endless and wondrous offerings for her to choose from.

But she'd made a grave error in judgment.

She'd stepped into her new world with her hair tumbling down her back, light makeup on her smiling face, wearing snug, comfortable jeans.

And there they were, the young men, waiting to pounce, wishing to have the beautiful ornament named Janice on their arm as testimony to their superior masculinity.

Once again, no one bothered to look beneath the surface, to get to know the person inside.

And so, even before the first semester ended, Janice Jennings disappeared.

In her place, the new Janice materialized.

Wearing baggy sweatsuits, thick glasses, her hair captured in a tight bun, a closed expression on her once-smiling face, the new Janice was ignored by the male populace. They scratched their heads in confusion, wondering where beautiful Janice had gone, when she would be back.

But she'd never reappeared.

She'd buried herself in her studies, her focus, her purpose, clearly defined. The boutique she would name Sleeping Beauty became her hope, her dream, as she earned her degree in business management.

Step by step, it all took form, just as she'd planned.

And she'd accomplished it all entirely alone.

There had been no friends, no lovers, no dates, nor parties to attend. She was literally invisible to the crowds of students surrounding her.

She'd accepted, then came to cherish, the life she led, the solitary existence. It was hers. Under her control, her direction, *her terms*. The lessons learned from her mother, husband and the university students had held her in good stead.

And so it had been ever since.

"Enough of this," Janice said, plunking back down onto the sofa.

Why on earth was she wasting her mental energies traipsing down memory lane, when her total concentration was needed for the evening ahead?

"Okay, Taylor Sinclair," she said, lifting her chin. "Go for it. Do your worst. I'm geared up and ready, you accountant you."

With a decisive nod, Janice patted the bun at the nape of her neck, folded her hands primly in her lap, and waited for Taylor to arrive.

Taylor drove slowly along the meandering street, nodding in approval as he saw the large, well-maintained houses.

Classy neighborhood, he thought. Mega-money neighborhood. Well, he knew for a fact that Janice could afford to live in this neck of the woods.

Seeing the number that he was looking for posted on a mailbox at the edge of the street, Taylor drove into the driveway and turned off the ignition. He folded his arms on top of the steering wheel and swept his gaze over the house.

Very nice. If he was of the mind to own a home, which he wasn't, Janice's choice of residence would suit his taste.

However, he had yet to see how she'd decorated her abode. If the interior reflected her mode of dress, the rooms would hold dark, overstuffed furniture with those crocheted gizmos on the arms and backs.

There would be knickknacks set in every spare space and far too many dreary pictures on the walls.

Within ten minutes after walking through the front door he'd be suffering from claustrophobia.

"Grim," he said, pulling the key free and opening the car door.

He made his way across the wide front yard on the round stepping stones nestled in the white gravel landscaping.

This dinner meeting with Janice had been on his mind a good portion of the day, though he hadn't found himself looking forward to it, nor dreading it. It had simply been there, popping into his thoughts at regular intervals.

He had a sneaking suspicion that he'd subconsciously focused on the evening ahead rather than the unsettling and nonsensical emotions Brandon Hamilton's lecture had produced.

What he'd experienced in his office the previous afternoon was *not* something he'd wish to repeat.

But there was a small chance of that. He'd gotten a solid night's sleep, exhaustion being all that had been wrong with him in the first place.

Centering his thoughts on Janice once again, Taylor stopped in front of the door and pressed the bell, hearing it chime inside the house.

Janice jumped to her feet, her heart racing as the doorbell rang. She hadn't been aware of a car arriving, but obviously Taylor was here.

Oh, dear heaven, Taylor was here.

"Stop it right now," she told herself. "You're calm, cool and collected. There is not a man standing at your front door, there is an accountant. Got that? Good.''

She marched across the living room and flung open the door.

Shoulders a block wide, legs long and powerful, rugged features bronzed by the sun, Taylor Sinclair was most definitely a man…an absolutely magnificent man.

No, no, no, Janice thought frantically. Taylor was an—

''Hello, Janice,'' Taylor said, smiling. ''You have a lovely—''

''Accountant,'' she said, then inwardly groaned as she felt a flush of embarrassment stain her cheeks.

''…home,'' Taylor said, frowning in confusion.

''I'm sorry,'' Janice said, raising both hands. ''Could we start over? Hello, Taylor, would you like to come in?'' She stepped back and managed to produce a small smile.

Taylor entered the house, took two steps, then stopped dead in his tracks. He started forward again slowly, scrutinizing all that was within his view.

Janice closed the door and watched Taylor as he visually examined her house. The butterflies increased their fluttering in her stomach, and she frowned in self-annoyance.

He was the first person, other than Shirley and Clem, to be invited over the threshold of her cherished domain, but she didn't care diddly what Taylor's reaction to her home was. She didn't want, nor need, his approval.

She was hardly breathing as she awaited his response.

"This is sensational," Taylor said, turning to look at Janice. "I really like what you've done in here. It's open, airy, yet still homey and welcoming."

The butterflies were pushed into oblivion by a swirling warmth that suffused her. "Thank you, Taylor," she said, unable to curb a genuine smile. "I still have a great deal of decorating to do, but I'm pleased with what I've accomplished so far."

"As well you should be," he said, nodding. He glanced around again. "If this was mine, I wouldn't change a thing. I would be very comfortable in this room."

"You would?" He would? Taylor could settle in, put his feet up and feel at home? Fancy that. "Well, I have yet to decide on what I want for the walls. I only have one picture of hummingbirds. It's hanging over my bed."

Taylor snapped to attention and looked directly into Janice's blue eyes.

Over her bed? his mind echoed. That slide-it-right-in-there statement made by one of the women he dated would be an invitation to proceed to the bedroom on the pretense of seeing the picture of the hummingbirds. The exit from said room would take place hours later.

But this was Janice. There was no coy, sexual

message in her eyes, on her face, to indicate she had been implying anything other than telling him where she happened to have hung the only picture she'd purchased thus far for her home.

It was as though Janice had emerged from another era, a time of honesty and innocence. She didn't play the swinging singles game, because she didn't know how!

She needed someone to protect her, to watch over her. She couldn't announce to every Tom, Dick and Harry that she had a picture of birds hanging above her *bed*, for cripe's sake.

Well, Janice was safe with him. Nobody would get within ten feet of her while he—

Taylor tore his gaze from Janice's mesmerizing eyes and cleared his throat.

He'd felt them again, the rushing emotions of protectiveness and possessiveness. And he was also painfully aware of the coiling heat low in his body produced by gazing too long into those incredible eyes of hers.

"Taylor?" Janice said, pushing her glasses up with one finger. "Is something wrong? You're looking at me as though I have a bug on my chin or something."

"Don't those heavy glasses make your nose hurt?" he said. Where in the hell had *that* come from? "Never mind. It's none of my business."

Janice removed the glasses and pinched the bridge of her nose.

"As a matter of fact," she said, "I suffer from

tired-nose syndrome.'' She smiled, shrugged, and started to put the glasses back in place.

''Wait.'' Taylor eased the glasses from Janice's hand. ''What do you need these for tonight? I'll be driving, so you don't have to worry about that.'' He held the glasses up to the light and peered through them. ''Are they for close work? I can tell you what's on the menu at the...'' His voice trailed off and he frowned.

Oh, no, Janice thought, feeling the color drain from her face. Where was that genie when she needed him? She wished... Oh, saints above...she wished she'd never taken off her glasses because Taylor was about to say...

''There's no prescription in these,'' he said, then looked at Janice again. ''This is clear glass, Janice.''

''Yes, well, yes, it certainly is, isn't it?''

Janice averted her eyes from Taylor's intense gaze and picked an imaginary thread from the lapel of her jacket.

''Why?'' he said. ''Why do you wear these things if you don't need them?''

A flash of anger rushed through Janice and she looked up at Taylor.

''More to the point,'' she said coolly, ''is why you believe it's any of your business, Mr. Sinclair. May I have my glasses back, please?''

''No.'' He squinted into space.

Janice planted her hands on her hips. ''Now what are you doing?''

"I'm thinking of an answer to your question as to why this is any of my business," he said. "Shh. I'm concentrating."

He was concentrating, all right, Taylor thought, but on far more than the question at hand. He was also zeroing in on regaining control of his body, and the spiraling heat that had rocketed through it at the sight of Janice without the heavy-framed glasses crowding her face.

She was even more lovely than he'd already concluded. The glasses had obscured the overall picture he could now see.

Sensational. Janice Jennings was, without a doubt, one of the most exquisitely beautiful women he'd ever had the pleasure of feasting his eyes upon.

"Allow me to assist you," Janice said, an angry edge still ringing in her voice. "Try the old saying, 'Men don't make passes at women who wear glasses.'"

"Aha," Taylor said. "So that's it." He waved the glasses in the air. "You're hiding behind these things." And the way she dressed? Was her total appearance her attempt to keep men at bay? That, he didn't know for certain. Yet. "Right?"

"I'm not *hiding*," she said, crossing her arms beneath her breasts. "That sounds very childish. I'm simply a woman who can't be bothered with the testosterone-induced antics men go through when they encounter a pretty face."

"Then you admit that you're pretty?" Taylor said, raising his eyebrows.

"Oh, for Pete's sake," she said, nearly yelling as she flung out her arms, "who are you now? My shrink? This conversation is ridiculous. Give me my glasses and let's go to dinner. I'm hungry."

"Let's see if I have this straight," Taylor said. "You're suffering from tired-nose syndrome from wearing glasses you don't need. That's not good, not good at all. That's very bad."

"Oh, pray tell, why?" she said.

"Because we have some heavy-duty things to discuss tonight regarding the future of Sleeping Beauty. You can't devote yourself to said discussion if a part of you is tired. In this case, your nose."

"You're totally bonkers, you know that."

"I'll ignore that," Taylor said. "This is very sound reasoning I'm presenting here."

"I—"

"Moving right along," he said, moving right along. "Your theory about lack of passes due to wearing these glasses produces the possibility that if you don't wear these things this evening, you'll still be unable to devote your entire brain power to our discussion because you'll be wondering if I'm going to make a pass at you. Correct?"

"I—"

"So we need to get that concern out of the way." Taylor walked to an end table, put down the glasses, then returned to stand in front of Janice. "Immediately."

"I—"

"Shh. I'm a dedicated accountant who always has the welfare of clients first and foremost in my mind. You need to be at your one hundred percent best to weigh and measure what I intend to propose for Sleeping Beauty. Therefore…"

Janice's eyes widened in shock as Taylor cradled her face in his large hands, lowered his head and brushed his lips over hers.

Once…

She stood ramrod stiff, her eyes as wide as saucers.

Twice…

A shiver coursed through her, followed by heat, consuming heat. Her lashes drifted down.

Then Taylor captured her mouth in a searing kiss that stole the very breath from her body and caused her heart to race in a wild, uneven tempo.

Oh, my stars, Janice thought, her bones were dissolving. This kiss was…divine.

Her hands floated up to rest on Taylor's shoulders as she savored the feel, the taste, the very essence of the kiss.

She was woman.

And, dear heaven, what an unbelievable kiss she was sharing with this magnificent man.

Man? her mind whispered. *No, no, no, this is not a man. This is an accountant.*

Janice's eyes flew open and she flattened her hands, pushing Taylor away.

"How dare you?" she said, then took a shuddering breath. "You have a lot of nerve, do you know that?"

No, Taylor thought, taking a much-needed breath. What he had was a body going up in flames.

Janice's lips had been beckoning to him from the first moment he'd seen her. He hadn't arrived at her door with the intention of kissing her, but now he *had* kissed her.

And because of that kiss, he wanted her, desired her beyond reason, ached for her to the point of pain in his aroused body.

"Well, there we go," he said, aware that his voice had the gritty quality of sandpaper. "The pass is out of the way so we've cleared the decks for a productive dinner meeting." He smiled. "Shall we go?"

Janice shot him the fiercest glare she could muster up, marched to the sofa to grab her purse, then headed for the front door.

"You are *not* your father's son," she said, poking her not-tired nose in the air. "Clem Sinclair is a gentleman."

Taylor chuckled and followed Janice out of the house.

The thick-framed glasses remained forgotten on the end table.

Chapter Five

With every mile that Taylor's sleek sports car covered as he drove away from Janice's house, the nearly palpable sexual tension within the vehicle increased. It hummed in the air, weaving around Janice and Taylor with invisible, crackling threads.

Taylor's hold on the steering wheel tightened to the point that his knuckles were white.

Janice shifted restlessly in the soft leather bucket seat, and she attempted several times to push glasses, which weren't there, higher on her nose.

They slid glances at each other, the remembrance of the kiss shared becoming more vivid, taunting them, as the heat of desire was fanned hotter and hotter within them.

"Janice..."

"Taylor…"

They had spoken in unison, then stopped, waiting for the other to continue.

Taylor took a deep breath, then exhaled slowly.

"Janice, look," he said, glancing over at her quickly, then redirecting his attention to the surging traffic. "I know I should apologize for what happened, for kissing you, but I can't, because I'm not sorry. That's as honest as I can be.

"If I could turn back the clock to that moment, I'd do it again…kiss you. If you want to fire me as your accountant, that's up to you."

"I see," Janice said quietly. "Well, no, I don't intend to fire you. As for the kiss…I was angry, but that's not really fair, because I shared that kiss with you, and while I don't know why it happened, I have to admit that I'm not sorry, either, that it did."

"Good," Taylor said, nodding. "That's good." He paused. "You don't know why I kissed you?"

"No, not really."

"You don't have any idea how…how kissable your lips are?"

Janice sighed wearily. "It's been brought to my attention in the past. Was that it, Taylor? I have pretty lips, so what the heck, why not kiss them?"

"No!" he yelled, causing Janice to jerk around in surprise at his outburst. "Sorry. I didn't mean to shout at you, but, cripe, that was a tacky thing to say. What do you think I do, walk down the street staring at women's lips, then kiss the ones that appeal to me?''

"I guess not," she said, then laughed suddenly. "That would result in your being in jail, instead of driving toward a restaurant right now."

"That's for sure," he said, smiling. "I'd definitely be in the clink, or out cold on the sidewalk somewhere because a woman decked me."

"I like that scenario even better," she said, laughing again.

"Thanks a lot."

Taylor looked over at Janice and they exchanged matching smiles before he returned his attention to the traffic. Several minutes went by in what slowly became a comfortable silence.

"I think," Janice said finally, "that we're being quite mature about this. We shared a kiss. It's over, done, finished. And, of course, it won't be repeated. We're back to our proper roles of accountant and client, and we'll have a business discussion during dinner regarding Sleeping Beauty and—"

"Hold it," Taylor interrupted, raising one hand. "Back up here."

"To where?"

"To the part where you said the kiss wouldn't be repeated. We both enjoyed it, so why wouldn't we do it again?"

"Oh, Taylor, come on. So I have pretty lips. Big deal. A multitude of women in this world have pretty lips. A multitude of women, I might add, who are more than willing to go further than just a kiss.

"I'm not your type, Taylor. You know that as well as I do. In appearance and mind-set, I am not the kind of woman you're accustomed to associating with."

"Oh? How do you know that?"

"I know," Janice said, nodding decisively. "Believe me, I know."

"You make me sound like a bed-hopping hustler," he said, his volume rising again.

"No, you're a man who moves in the singles scene and who dates women in said singles scene. You play by those rules. I do not. It's very simple really. We have absolutely nothing in common, don't operate on the same wavelength. Therefore, we're not going to share any more kisses. That's the end of the story."

"You're very quick to label people, Janice. You could be wrong, you know."

"But I'm not. Don't make this more complicated than it should be. It's getting borderline ridiculous as it is. Our kiss is becoming the most thoroughly discussed kiss in the history of kisses.

"From now on, view me as a client, not a woman. I'll view you as an accountant, not a man." Janice shrugged. "And that, as they say, is that."

"Mmm," Taylor said, frowning.

Janice was right, he thought. Damn it, he didn't want her to be right. But, yes, she was right. She *wasn't* even close to being his type.

"I'll give some serious thought to what you said," Taylor said.

"I'd prefer to hear that you thoroughly agree with me, Taylor."

"I'll keep you posted."

Janice rolled her eyes heavenward.

"So, tell me, Ms. Jennings," Taylor said, striving for a casual tone of voice. "Do you do anything else besides wearing phony glasses to keep men at arm's length?"

He was pushing her, and he knew it. He was running the risk of making Janice so angry she'd demand he turn the car around and take her home.

But he wanted to know, needed to know, if Janice's mode of dress was a calculated maneuver on her part. It was an important piece of the puzzle that had to be put in place so he could understand Janice better, come closer to knowing who she really was.

Why did it matter that he figure out what was going on in that complicated female mind of hers? Hell, he didn't know.

"Well?" he said.

"The glasses have managed to accomplish a great deal," she said.

Not bad, Janice, she told herself. She'd answered Taylor's question, which was really none of his business in the first place, without telling a bold-faced lie. She had no intention of admitting that she purposely dressed in a less-than-attractive manner.

That statement would produce more questions,

and begin to unravel the layers of her past, exposing all she wished to forget.

"Just the glasses," Taylor said thoughtfully.

"Mmm."

Taylor's silence seemed to suggest he didn't fully believe her.

"Here's the restaurant," he said, turning into a curving driveway. "Still hungry?"

"Famished," she said.

And more than ready to have this conversation ended once and for all, she thought firmly. She'd stated in no uncertain terms that from here on out, she and Taylor were client and accountant, strictly business. He was intelligent enough to get the message.

And her own assignment? Somehow, dear heaven, she had to erase the memory of that kiss shared with Taylor. Forget the taste and feel and pure ecstasy of his lips on hers, and the heated desire that had consumed her. Somehow.

The restaurant was one of the city's finest. The tables were arranged to afford maximum privacy for the diners by utilizing tall, folding silk screens with delicate flowers painted on them.

Janice complimented Taylor on his selection of where they would dine and he gave the credit to his father, saying Clem had recommended the establishment as an excellent place to have a private business discussion.

They were led to their table by the hostess, who

placed large menus on the linen table-cloth and said a waiter would be with them shortly.

As Taylor was assisting Janice with her chair, a couple in their early sixties appeared at the edge of the screen.

"Taylor?" the woman said. "Yes, I thought that was you. How are you, dear? And how is Clem? We've been on a cruise and have just returned."

"Hello, Mildred. Charles," Taylor said, smiling. "Dad is grumbling about being retired. I guess it's going to take him a while to adjust to the idle hours."

Any second now, Janice thought, Mr. Socially Perfect Sinclair would, of course, introduce her to Mildred and Charles. Any second now.

And he would make it very clear that Ms. Janice Jennings was a client and that they were about to engage in a *business* discussion over dinner.

Oh, yes, he'd make that crystal clear, because heaven forbid that Mildred and Charles would pass the word that Taylor Sinclair was losing his touch, had been seen in the company of a less-than-stunning woman.

"Mildred, Charles," Taylor said, from where he stood behind Janice's chair, "I'd like you to meet Janice Jennings."

Janice jerked in her chair as she felt Taylor's hands settle onto her shoulders.

"Janice, this is Mildred and Charles Hunt. They've been friends of my family for as long as I can remember."

And? Janice prompted. Whip it on 'em, Taylor. Give 'em the spiel about the accountant and client business dinner.

"It's a pleasure to meet you, Janice," Mildred said, smiling.

"Indeed," Charles said.

"I...um...yes, it's nice to make your acquaintance," Janice said, producing a small smile.

That was it? she thought, totally confused. Taylor wasn't going to explain why he was with her in this exclusive and very romantic environment? What was the matter with him? This didn't make one bit of sense.

"Well, we'll leave you to enjoy yourselves," Mildred said.

"I'll give Clem a call soon," Charles said, "and see if he wants to get together. I'm surviving retirement. He'll get the hang of it."

Taylor laughed. "Just don't suggest he take up golf if you value your life."

"All right, I'll keep that in mind," Charles said, smiling.

After an exchange of goodbyes, the Hunts disappeared behind the screen. Taylor dropped his hands from Janice's shoulders, moved around the table and settled onto his chair. He picked up the menu.

"Well, let's see what they're offering us," he said, looking at Janice. "Is something wrong? Now *you're* staring at *me* as though I have a bug on my chin."

"What?" Janice blinked. "Oh, no, nothing is wrong. I just..." She grabbed the menu and gave it her undivided attention. "Hungry, very hungry."

Taylor shook his head slightly, then looked at the dinner selections.

He'd obviously missed something here, he thought. Women. God love 'em, they really were very complicated creatures.

Men, Janice thought, mentally shaking her head. They were so complex and unpredictable.

The wine steward appeared at the table and Taylor made a selection.

During the ongoing interruptions of tasting and approving the wine, ordering their dinners and having crisp salads placed in front of them, Janice and Taylor chatted about the decor of the restaurant, a bestselling novel everyone was raving about but neither had had time to read, and the rapidly approaching summer heat.

"Do you have a swimming pool at your house?" Taylor said, then took a bite of salad.

Janice nodded. "I use it a great deal. It's very refreshing, plus it satisfies my conscience about exercising. I swim a few laps and tell myself I don't qualify as a couch potato."

Taylor chuckled, then popped a cherry tomato into his mouth.

Janice Jennings in a bathing suit, he mused. Maybe she had gone to one of those novelty shops that sold vintage clothes and purchased an old-fashioned suit with long sleeves and bloomers.

Or maybe she wore an enormous T-shirt when she swam.

Or a large pair of cotton pajamas.

Well, one thing was for sure. Since he liked living, he wasn't going to ask Janice what style swimsuit she had, or what she did with her hair when in the pool. He'd just sit there and quietly die of curiosity.

Their dinners arrived piping hot and smelling heavenly. Janice had chosen shrimp scampi, while Taylor was ready to tackle a thick steak. They ate in silence for several minutes.

"Delicious," Janice said finally.

"I'm glad you're enjoying it," Taylor said. "This steak is great, too." He paused. "Janice, I'm going to ask you a question, and if you'd prefer not to answer it that's fine. Fair enough?"

Janice stiffened in her chair. "Yes, I guess so. What…what do you want to know?"

Damn it, Taylor fumed at himself. Janice had begun to relax, had been chatting, smiling freely and often, and now look at what he'd done. Her expression was guarded, and her beautiful and expressive eyes were radiating a message of wariness.

But it was too late to erase what he'd said, so he might as well go for it.

Looking directly at her, he said, "Why do you keep your ownership of Sleeping Beauty a secret?"

A rush of relief swept through Janice, causing her to smile.

Thank goodness, she thought. She'd been so

afraid that Taylor was going to plow right in and ask her why she downplayed her womanly attributes, her femininity. *That* topic was taboo, one she had no intention of ever discussing with anyone.

"It's very simple, really," she said with a little shrug. "Didn't your father explain it to you?"

"He said he didn't know."

"Oh." Janice frowned. "Well, now that I think about it, I guess Clem never asked. He just accepted the arrangement."

Taylor smiled. "My father is more polite than I am. I'm definitely asking."

Janice took a bite of the fluffy, baked potato on her plate before speaking again.

"During the first six months that Sleeping Beauty was open," she said quietly, "I was besieged by salesmen from a multitude of companies. They wanted to wine and dine me, sent me flowers, brought me gifts from their inventories, and on and on."

Taylor nodded. "That's standard operating procedure. It's part of the perks of starting up what was obviously a classy store."

"I didn't view it that way, Taylor. Those men were prepared to spend time with me, spare no expense, ooze phony charm and faked interest in every little thing I said.

"But it wasn't because I was a nice woman, who was pleasant to be with. It was due to the fact that I had something they wanted...a lucrative account for their companies."

She shook her head.

"I refused to be manipulated that way, used for others' benefit. I began to tell the salesmen to leave their samples, that I would meet with the owner and get back to them later. Once they understood that I was only the manager, the invitations to go out on the town, the flowers and gifts, stopped cold."

"I see," Taylor said.

"Do you?" she said, leaning slightly toward him. "*I* control my life, Taylor. No one, *no one,* uses me to obtain what *they* are after for *their* ultimate goals. I will never again be a helpless marionette, whose strings are pulled by…"

Janice's voice trailed off and she sank back in her chair.

"I'm sorry," she said. "I got carried away." She patted her lips with her napkin, averting her eyes from Taylor's. "Anyway, that's the story. I will remain in the role of manager of Sleeping Beauty. It has worked out very well and will continue to do so."

The waiter appeared to top up their water glasses, giving Taylor an opportunity to digest Janice's vehement answer to his question.

He wasn't buying it, he thought. Not for a second. He could understand to a point Janice's aversion to being fawned over by the droves of phony, means-to-an-end salesmen.

But there was a lot more going on here than that. He'd seen the shadow of pain in Janice's eyes during her dissertation. Someone, or maybe more than one someone, had used and abused her in some manner in the past.

There were walls...yes, protective walls around her that she'd no doubt carefully constructed, that were bigger and stronger than just a pair of unflattering glasses.

Janice wasn't just keeping men at arm's length, she held the world at bay, not trusting nor believing in anyone who crossed her path.

A surge of hot fury consumed him.

Who had done this to Janice? What exactly had she been subjected to, and when had it all happened? Oh, man, he'd like to get his hands on whoever was responsible for hurting her.

And what was it going to take to get Janice to lower those walls of hers, to trust and believe in *him?*

Whoa, Sinclair, he thought. An even more appropriate question was, why it mattered so much to him that Janice knew that she could trust him.

Hell, he sure didn't know the answer to *that* one. Well, he'd concentrate on the *why* later. At the moment, his concern was how to chip away at those protective walls of Janice's.

Trust me, Janice, Taylor thought dryly. Yeah, right. That was a cliché, would cause the women he knew to fall apart laughing at the absurdity of such a dumb statement. It was an old, overused line in the singles scene.

It was going to take action, not words, to gain Janice's trust. Okay, what kind of action? Man, oh, man, he was treading on foreign territory here. He'd never met anyone like Janice before. He didn't have the foggiest idea as to what he was doing.

Think, Sinclair. Well, if he wanted Janice to trust him he had to give her something in return, something to hold on to.

Honesty.

He had to be absolutely, one hundred percent, flat out honest with her at all times.

"Janice," he said.

She pushed the food around on her plate, not raising her head to respond.

"I just want you to know," Taylor said, "that I would never attempt to take advantage of you or… What I mean is, I wouldn't treat you like a…a marionette or… I'm trying to say that you're…that I'm… Well, hell, I'm a complete fumble mouth here." He paused. "Would you look at me, please?"

Janice shifted her gaze slowly from her plate to look directly into Taylor's eyes. He nearly groaned aloud when he saw the lingering shadows of pain still reflected in her expressive blue eyes.

He reached over and covered one of her hands with his where it rested on the top of the table.

"I'm trying to avoid telling you that you can trust me," he said quietly. "But I'm doing a lousy job of finding another way to put it."

"Taylor, I—"

"No, don't say anything. I don't expect you to

believe me right off the bat. Just give me a chance to prove it to you.''

''Why? I *trust* you as my accountant, but you're speaking about more than that, aren't you? Why, Taylor?''

''I don't know. I honestly don't know.'' Taylor shook his head. ''It's important to me, that's all I'm certain of right now. You've obviously been hurt very badly in the past, and I have no intention of being on the list with those who caused you pain.

''Give me a chance to know you better. Don't shut me out. Don't hide behind your protective walls, refuse to see who *I* really am. Okay?''

No! Janice's mind screamed. *No! It's too dangerous. Taylor is dangerous. The whole scenario he's proposing is dangerous. No!*

Taylor began to stroke her wrist with his thumb, as he continued to look directly into her eyes.

Heat traveled up Janice's arm and danced across her breasts, causing them to feel heavy, aching for a soothing touch.

The heat increased, swirling lower in her body, lower, beginning to pulse in the same steady tempo as Taylor's thumb on her soft skin.

She couldn't breathe.

She couldn't think.

Oh, dear heaven, what was this man doing to her?

''Janice?'' Taylor said. ''Will you do it? Give

me a chance to be a man in your life, as well as your accountant?''

No! she thought frantically.

''Yes,'' she heard herself whisper.

Chapter Six

The waiter materialized from behind the screen to discuss the dessert menu and Janice nearly flung her arms around the man in gratitude. She jerked her hand free from beneath Taylor's.

"Janice?" Taylor said.

"No. No, thank you," she said, looking everywhere except at Taylor.

"How about coffee and brandy?" he said.

"What? Oh, yes, that would be fine." Janice pushed back her chair and got to her feet. "Excuse me. I'll be right back." She snatched her purse from the floor and hurried away.

Taylor placed the order, the waiter nodded, then disappeared. A young girl appeared a few moments later and began to remove the dinner dishes. Taylor leaned back in his chair to get out of the way, his thoughts centered on Janice.

Ms. Jennings was jangled, he mused. She'd literally bolted out of their cubbyhole, having managed not to meet his gaze again after agreeing to allow him a role in her life other than just being her accountant.

Janice, he assumed, was attempting to soothe her rattled state of mind in the ladies' room. What was she thinking? Would she return to the table and announce that she'd reconsidered? That he was once again not a man, but only an accountant?

Taylor narrowed his eyes.

No way, lovely Janice. A deal was a deal, and he was going to hold her to it.

Now what? Well, he should put into motion opportunities to see Janice, to be with her, beyond discussing the financial future of Sleeping Beauty.

But he'd have to take this slow and easy. Janice was like a skittish colt, a timid, wounded little bird, a—

Enough of the cute metaphors, Sinclair.

While he had this time alone, he should be asking himself why he was doing this, why he'd been so determined to get Janice to agree to expand his place in her life.

And why he'd felt a surge of pure joy when she'd whispered the "yes" that he'd been barely able to hear.

But he didn't know the answers to those nagging questions.

All he knew was that they *mattered,* more than he could even begin to explain to himself.

You could be lonely even as we speak and not even know it.

"Oh, no, you don't, Hamilton," Taylor said under his breath as Brandon's words echoed in his mind.

Wanting to be with Janice did not, in any way, indicate that he was lonely, that he was hoping she would fill some void in his existence.

That was absurd.

He was not lonely!

His life was exactly the way he wanted it.

His momentary preoccupation with Janice Jennings was due to…yes, okay, it was coming to him now…due to her being like no woman he'd ever met before. She intrigued him, was a challenging puzzle he intended to solve.

Did that sound tacky?

No, it was rational reasoning.

Did he want Janice to trust him in order to satisfy a rush of male ego by being the one to get beyond those protective walls of hers?

Now *that* would definitely be tacky.

Taylor shook his head.

No, this wasn't a game he was playing based on an overdose of machismo.

Janice had touched him deep inside in a place that was new, foreign, to him. A knot had tightened in his gut when he saw the pain in her beautiful eyes, and fury had rushed through him like hot, molten lava.

One truth was crystal clear.

He would never do anything to hurt Janice Jennings.

In the powder room, Janice ran her hands under cold water. She stared at the wrist where Taylor's thumb had stroked in that maddening rhythm, having the strange sense that the soft skin belonged to someone else.

It was still warm, she thought incredulously. The water was becoming icy cold and she could still feel the heat, the incredible heat, that had traveled throughout her entire body from the caress of Taylor's thumb.

Janice turned off the water, dried her hands, disposed of the paper towel, then finally forced herself to meet her own gaze in the mirror.

"What have you done?" she said softly, hearing the trembling in her voice and seeing the pallor of her cheeks.

In one heart-stopping moment, when she'd said the tiny word "yes," she'd shaken the very structure of her existence.

The protective walls she'd so carefully constructed around herself years before were teetering, threatening to crumble into dust, leaving her exposed and vulnerable.

"I can't do this," she said, unwelcome tears misting her eyes. "It's too dangerous, too..."

Stop it, she ordered herself in the next instant. She was no longer a child. She was a woman. She was in charge, in control. She was retreating back in time to when she didn't have the strength, nor the wisdom, to keep from being manipulated, used for others's gain.

Well, that was then and this is now.

She didn't know why Taylor Sinclair was so determined that she allow him to be more in her life than just her accountant. She didn't have the foggiest idea what his motives were.

But, darn it, she could handle this.

No matter what was brewing in Taylor's complicated, male mind, he couldn't take advantage of her in any way, shape or form, because she simply wouldn't allow it.

However, for a short length of time—for Taylor would lose interest in her very quickly, of course—she might actually step into the world of "dating," looking just as she did now, *on her terms.*

Yes, that would be nice.

Perhaps they'd dine again in a fancy restaurant like this one. Or attend a concert. Or go on a picnic.

Janice watched her smiling reflection in the mirror.

It had been so many years since she'd gone anywhere with a man. It would be a pleasant interlude, hours stolen out of time.

If he attempted to seduce her, hustle her into bed, he'd grow weary, perhaps even angry, at her constant refusals.

Janice laughed. "You're dreaming, silly person."

A man like Taylor Sinclair would have no desire to make love with someone who looked like she did. There was nothing alluring about the way she presented herself.

But that realization brought her right back to the extremely confusing question of why Taylor was so determined to be viewed as a man in her eyes, instead of just her accountant.

"Beats me," she said, shrugging. "I don't know. I don't care."

With a decisive nod, she spun around and left the powder room.

Janice slid back onto her chair at the table just as the waiter was leaving after delivering cups of coffee and snifters of brandy.

"I timed that perfectly, didn't I?" she said, smiling. "Now then, Taylor, don't you think we should discuss whatever is on your mind regarding Sleeping Beauty? We'll be here until the restaurant closes if we don't get down to business. You have the floor, Mr. Sinclair."

Interesting, Taylor thought, looking at Janice intently. Whatever Janice had talked over with herself in the ladies' room had resulted in her now being calm, cool and collected.

It was becoming difficult as hell to keep up with this woman!

But so be it. A smiling Janice was far better than

the upset Janice who had practically run from the table.

"Taylor?"

"Oh, yes, the subject of Sleeping Beauty," he said, snapping back to attention. "Okay, here it is. You have far too much money sitting in the bank earning very low interest. Those profit monies are costing you a bundle in taxes, too. You need to invest in something that will reduce your taxable income."

Janice took a sip of coffee, then replaced the china cup on the saucer.

"Such as?" she said. "I've told you that I've expanded as much as possible in my present location. It would be foolish to move from where my customer base expects to find me."

"That's true. I'm proposing a location in addition to the one you now have."

"Oh, I don't think—"

"Just hear me out, all right?" Taylor interrupted. "This is a very unique opportunity and would be perfect for you. Will you listen with an open mind?"

"Yes. Certainly. Proceed."

"Good. I grew up in Prescott, and so did a close friend of mine named Brandon Hamilton."

Taylor explained the restoration of Hamilton House, the success the hotel was enjoying, and Brandon and Andrea's plans for adding specialty shops in the lobby of the grand old hotel.

"I spoke with Brandon today," he went on, "and

the architect has presented some dynamite plans, incorporating a lot of Andrea's ideas. There will be a narrow cobblestone walkway in front of the shops, with old-fashioned lampposts. The stores will be small, of course, but with carefully selected inventories.''

Janice nodded as she felt a bubble of excitement begin to grow within her.

"It sounds charming," she said. "Like a turn of the century village to match the Victorian decor of the hotel you described."

"Exactly," Taylor said, leaning toward her slightly. "Brandon and Andrea are being very careful about who they're inviting to come in there. The shops must be exclusive, classy and expensive. Sleeping Beauty most definitely qualifies.

"They would be in a position to get potential managers for you to interview from people Brandon knows. Andrea would handle the advertising as she has started her own firm in Prescott. Would that be a problem with the agency you have a contract with now?''

"No, not at all. I have a clause that limits my obligation to them to my Phoenix store. I put that in the contract at the last minute, although I really don't know why."

Taylor smiled. "Maybe you have a crystal ball you weren't aware of." He paused. "Listen, this is Tuesday. How would you feel about driving up to Prescott with me on Saturday and looking things over? Brandon and Andrea would like to meet you, too, and see some samples of your merchandise.''

"Well," Janice said slowly, "I... Yes, all right. I don't work the weekends at Sleeping Beauty. My staff covers Saturday and Sunday."

"Great. We'll stay overnight."

Janice blinked. "Pardon me?"

"Since Brandon grew up in Prescott, he knows so many people that he and Andrea decided to postpone their wedding reception until the weather would allow a big shindig on the town square.

"They've been so busy with the plans for the shops in the hotel, they just didn't get around to checking with the Chamber of Commerce to see when the square would be free for them to use it."

"Free of what?" Janice said.

"Craft shows, art exhibits, that sort of thing. They have to put together their reception for this Sunday since it's the only open date left on the calendar."

"And?" Janice said, frowning.

"Well, we do Sleeping Beauty business on Saturday and attend the party on Sunday. The hotel was booked solid, but they had one cancellation. You can have that room, and I'll bunk on Andrea and Brandon's sofa. They live in the hotel. Or I'll sleep on the aunts' sofa." Taylor chuckled. "They'd pamper and feed me...big time."

"The aunts?"

"Aunt Prudence and Aunt Charity, Brandon's great-aunts. They're twins, but they're as different as day and night. They're dear old ladies, and you'll love 'em.''

"Taylor, I realize that you wish to attend the wedding reception, but I'm not certain I'd feel comfortable crashing the party. Why don't we drive up in separate cars, and I'll come back on Saturday?"

"Hey, no way. Brandon specifically said to be sure you knew you were invited to the party. Say yes, Janice. We'll combine business with pleasure. It'll be fun.''

Fun? How many years had it been since she'd had some honest-to-goodness fun? More than she could remember.

But, gracious, an entire weekend in the company of Taylor Sinclair? Was that smart? Or was it dangerous beyond belief?

Don't panic, she told herself. She was in charge, in control, remember? She…could…handle…this!

"All right, Taylor," she said, smiling. "I agree to your proposal.''

"You do?" he said, surprise evident on his face. "I was gearing up to talk until I was blue in the face to convince you to—Hey, I'm not complaining." He lifted the brandy snifter. "Here's to the weekend in Prescott, and to all it may bring.''

Janice narrowed her eyes. "Meaning?"

"Your expanding Sleeping Beauty into Hamilton House isn't a done deal. You have to like what you see, and Brandon and Andrea have to decide if your merchandise meets their criteria.''

"Oh, yes, of course. Yes.''

"Shall we toast to the weekend?"

Janice lifted her snifter and touched it gently against Taylor's.

"To the weekend," she said.

The butterflies were back, she thought a tad frantically. There they were, swooshing around in her stomach again.

She took a sip of the rich, smooth brandy.

Maybe that would put the butterflies to sleep. Goodness, the brandy was warming her right down to her toes. That was probably a good thing, because it wouldn't take much to get cold feet about this weekend.

She took another swallow of brandy.

No, by golly, she'd be fine. She'd conduct business for Sleeping Beauty on Saturday, then on Sunday she would indulge in some old-fashioned fun.

"Well, Taylor," she said, smiling. "What does one wear to a wedding reception on the town square in Prescott, Arizona?"

Easy does it, Taylor told himself. He'd better pick his words carefully to reply to that question.

"It will be very casual," he said. "You know, like a big picnic. Wear whatever you're comfortable in to sit on a blanket on the grass."

Janice nodded.

"I'm glad you've agreed to go for the entire weekend," he said quietly.

"I'm looking forward to it."

They exchanged smiles, gazing directly into each

other's eyes. Then their smiles faded as the heat of desire began to churn, build, pulse.

The remembrance of the kiss they'd shared in Janice's living room hummed in their minds and bodies.

Oh, dear heaven, Janice thought, she was being consumed by licking flames of heated passion that were like nothing she'd ever experienced before.

This was want and need in its purest and most honest form. This was Janice, the woman, desiring Taylor, the man, with an intensity beyond description.

How terribly dangerous this was, yet…yes, it was exciting, too, so very tantalizing, and new and wondrous. She was so alive and incredibly feminine.

Savor this, her mind whispered. She would tuck it away as a special memory, mark on a mental calendar the exact day, hour, minute she'd allowed her womanliness full rein as it awakened for this stolen moment.

But quickly now, she must return to who she was, who she must be to protect herself. Sleeping Beauty.

Janice tore her gaze from Taylor's and stared into the amber liquid in the brandy snifter.

Taylor sat perfectly still, willing his aroused body back under his command. A trickle of sweat ran down his chest and his heart was beating with a wild tempo that was quieting slowly.

Lord, he thought, taking a swallow of brandy.

How much time had passed while he was pinned in place by Janice's mesmerizing eyes?

The restaurant had seemed to fade into oblivion, to be replaced by an eerie, sensual mist that had surrounded them.

Heat had rocketed through him, burning, raging out of control.

He wanted Janice Jennings.

It was as simple and as complicated as that.

Even more mystifying was that he knew it wasn't just lust. It was more than that, much more.

There were emotions of protectiveness and possessiveness intertwined with his desire. Janice was so fragile, his little wounded bird, and he would protect and care for her, stand between her and harm's way.

No one would ever hurt her again, cause pain like that which he'd seen in her expressive eyes. *No one.*

Sinclair, you're losing it, he mentally fumed. He had to get back on track. Janice continually pushed his sensual buttons because...because she was so different from the women he knew.

She blindsided him. It wasn't exactly earth-shattering, it was simply new, like an uncharted course, a road he hadn't traveled down before.

There. That made sense.

But just to be on the safe side, he'd better end this outing before he leaped over the table, hauled Janice into his arms and kissed her senseless.

"Janice, are you ready?" he said, hearing the gritty quality of his voice.

Janice's head snapped up and her eyes widened. "What?"

"To leave," he added quickly. "Go home. We've covered everything we need to." And then some. "Shall we call it a night?" A night he had a sneaking feeling he wouldn't soon forget.

"Yes. Yes, of course." She leaned over and picked up her purse from the floor.

"I'll settle the check and we'll be on our way," Taylor said, attempting to produce a smile that didn't quite materialize.

"Fine," Janice said. "I want to thank you for the delicious dinner. Oh, and thank you for giving me and Sleeping Beauty so much thought, above and beyond the call of duty. I'm excited about the possibility of having a shop in Hamilton House. I hope I can reach an agreement that is satisfactory to Andrea, Brandon and me. Yes, it would be a sound business decision to—"

"Janice," Taylor interrupted.

She got to her feet. "I'll meet you in the lobby, Taylor."

As Janice disappeared around the edge of the screen, there was no doubt in Taylor's mind that the desire that had consumed him had staked a claim on Janice, too.

And that was a fact he would not, could not, take advantage of. Janice didn't play, nor even know, the rules of the game. She was off limits, not his to have, nor to make love with.

* * *

Darkness had fallen by the time Janice and Taylor left the restaurant, and the sky was a brilliant canopy of twinkling, diamond-like stars.

"Oh, my," Janice said, looking up at the spectacle of nature's beauty. "Isn't that gorgeous?"

Taylor stared at Janice's profile, seeing the gentle slope of her throat and the outline of her delicate features.

"Yes," he said quietly, still looking at Janice. "Beautiful. And not appreciated by those who don't take the time to really *see* what's actually there."

"Mmm," Janice said. "You're right."

The valet screeched to a halt in front of them, then jumped out of Taylor's car, beaming.

"Cool car, man," the boy said. He ran around the vehicle and opened the door for Janice. "Ma'am?"

Janice laughed softly as Taylor drove away from the restaurant.

"Ma'am?" she said. "That makes me feel ancient. That boy didn't look old enough to have a driver's license."

Taylor chuckled. "He's probably a student at Arizona State. The older I get, the younger everyone else appears to me."

"I know what you mean."

"My father is the one who is really having problems coming to grips with his age," Taylor said, his smile changing into a frown. "He's fighting this retirement thing. I've tried to tell him to give it a fair chance, because it has only been a few weeks.

"It worries me. If he doesn't have the proper attitude, he'll never adjust to his new life-style. He's also dwelling too much on missing my mother and she's been gone for fifteen years. He keeps thinking about the plans they had together for when he retired."

"I hope he'll learn to be content again," Janice said. "Clem is a very nice man, very special."

Taylor nodded. "That he is. He's aged a great deal in the past year or so, though. I can see the differences in him. His heart condition has taken its toll, I'm afraid."

"You love him very much, don't you?" Janice said, looking over at Taylor.

"Yes. Yes, I do." Taylor paused, glanced quickly at Janice, then redirected his attention to the heavy traffic. "What about you, Janice? Your family?"

"I'm an only child and I never knew my father. My mother said he died while attempting to rescue some people from a burning building, but I don't believe that.

"I don't think my parents were ever married. There were no photographs, no mementos of my father, and my mother didn't wear a wedding ring. She claimed it was too sad to see that ring on her finger, knowing he was gone."

"That sounds feasible to me," Taylor said, lifting one shoulder in a shrug.

"I suppose it does," she said. "But I remember one time when my mother said my father had drowned while trying to save some swimmers caught in an undertow. She didn't keep her lies straight."

"Oh, I see. Does that upset you?"

"I really don't care one way or the other."

"And your mother?" Taylor said. "Where is *she?*"

"She was killed in an automobile accident when I had just turned twenty. She was in a car with... Well, that's not important. She and...her companion had been drinking heavily. He...the driver...lost control of the car and slammed into a tree. They were both killed instantly."

"Lord, Janice, I'm sorry," Taylor said, frowning. "That's rough."

"There's nothing to be sorry about," she said, her voice flat and low. "People shouldn't drink and drive. What they did was wrong." She paused. "Very, *very* wrong."

And there was something *very wrong* with this story, Taylor thought, narrowing his eyes. There was a cold edge to Janice's voice that he'd never heard from her before.

She'd skittered around saying who was driving the car when the accident that had killed her mother occurred. There was definitely more to this tale than Janice was telling.

And now there was another piece missing from the puzzle that was Janice Jennings.

"So, you're all alone in this world," Taylor said. "What did you do on Christmas?"

"Christmas?" Janice said. "Where did that come from?"

"I don't know. Christmas is such a family-oriented day. I just wondered if you were alone."

"No, I celebrated with my neighbor, Shirley. She's divorced and has no children, so we cooked a nice dinner together and exchanged gifts. It was very pleasant. Good heavens, Taylor, don't view me as poor little orphan Annie. I'm very happy with my life exactly as it is."

You could be lonely even as we speak and not even know it.

Was Janice lonely? he thought. And not aware that she was, because she'd been on her own for so long? Deep within her, perhaps unknown even to herself, did she yearn for a soul mate, a husband, a baby?

Now he was sounding like Brandon. Janice had her life set up exactly the way she wanted it, just as he did.

But then again, maybe she didn't realize she was lonely because—

"Cripe," he said, shaking his head in self-disgust.

"What's wrong?"

"Oh. Nothing," he said. "I'm just not making any of the signal lights. They see me coming and turn red. But that's fine. We're in no rush."

"No," Janice said softly. "Not at all."

"We'll just take it slow and easy," Taylor said.

But what beautiful Janice didn't realize, he thought, was that he wasn't talking about how he was driving the car.

Chapter Seven

Janice crossed the dark living room to snap on a lamp, sending a soft glow of light over a portion of the large room. She turned to see that Taylor was still standing just inside the closed front door.

"Your keys," he said, extending them toward her.

"Yes, thank you." She retraced her steps and took the keys. "Could I offer you something to drink, Taylor? I'm afraid I don't have any liquor in the house, but I have soda, sun tea, or I could make a pot of coffee."

"No, thank you," he said, smiling. "The brandy and coffee did the trick."

"Oh. Well. All right." Janice paused. "Then I guess I'll see you on Saturday. What time would you like to leave?"

"Ten o'clock? That would get us up to Prescott at the lunch hour. We'll eat when we get there."

"Fine."

"Remember that it's a lot cooler a mile high, so bring a sweater."

"Fine," Janice said, nodding.

"Well, I guess I'll shove off."

"Fine."

Taylor frowned. "You sound like a broken record."

"Yes, I guess I do," she said, laughing. "Fine, fine, fine. That just goes to show you how easy I am to get along with."

"Yeah, right," Taylor said, chuckling and shaking his head. "If you leave out the fact that you're the most complicated woman I've ever met."

"Me?" Janice splayed one hand on her breasts, an expression of genuine surprise on her face.

"You, Ms. Jennings."

"Well, you're rather complex yourself, Mr. Sinclair," she said, smiling.

"You're kidding."

"Nope," she said, shaking her head.

"I don't suppose you'd like to sit down and have an in-depth discussion about all of this?" he said, raising his eyebrows.

"That would *not* be a good idea." Janice extended her right hand toward Taylor. "Thank you again for a lovely evening."

"The pleasure was mine."

Taylor looked at Janice's hand, her face, then

back at her hand. He gave it a quick shake, then started toward the door.

"Good night, Taylor," Janice said softly.

Taylor stood with his back to her, one hand on the doorknob. One second ticked by, then two, then three.

"Ah, hell," he said finally. "This is ridiculous."

He turned around, closed the short distance between them and cradled Janice's face in his hands. He gazed directly into her eyes for a long moment, then lowered his head and claimed her mouth with his.

Oh, thank goodness, Janice thought.

Taylor dropped his hands from her face to wrap his arms around her, nestling her close to his body. Her hands floated upward to encircle his neck, her fingertips inching into his thick hair.

He parted her lips to delve his tongue into her mouth, meeting her tongue in a stroking rhythm.

The kiss was ecstasy. It tasted of rich brandy, with a faint flavor of coffee. The kiss was heat exploding within them as desires soared. The kiss was theirs, and they savored every breath-stealing moment of it.

She didn't want this kiss ever to end. *That's my second wish, little genie,* Janice thought dreamily. Taylor felt so good, tasted so good, smelled so good, like soap and fresh air and man. He made her feel so feminine and alive. And so very, very special.

Taylor raised his head a fraction of an inch to

take a rough breath, then slanted his mouth in the opposite direction as his lips captured Janice's once again.

Nectar, he thought. Sweet nectar. Kissing Janice, having her pressed to his aroused body, was sending him up in flames. She was heaven in his arms, and he didn't want to let her go. She was responding to him, totally, passionately, and it made him feel ten feet tall.

Oh, Lord, how he wanted to make love with this woman.

The demanding voice of reason began to hammer at Taylor's mind, pushing its way through the sensual mist consuming him.

Slowly and reluctantly, he ended the kiss, gripped Janice by the shoulders and eased her away from his painfully aroused body.

Janice slid her arms slowly from Taylor's neck and met his gaze, seeing the heated desire smoldering in his dark eyes and knowing the same want and need was reflected in her own.

Taylor took a step backward, then drew one thumb gently over Janice's moist, slightly parted lips.

"I want you, Janice," he said, his voice gritty with passion. "And *you* want *me*. That's it, the *honest* bottom line. But I know, I just somehow know, that if we make love tonight, you'll regret it in the morning, and I couldn't handle that."

"I..." Janice started, then for the life of her couldn't think of another thing to say.

"When we *do* make love," Taylor went on, "the time will be right for both of us. That's the way it should be, has to be, because what we would share will be very, very rare and wonderful. So—" he brushed his lips over hers "—good night, Janice Jennings."

"Good night, Taylor Sinclair," she whispered.

Taylor left the house, closing the door behind him with a quiet click.

Janice didn't move. She simply stood staring at the door, her mind racing as her heart began to slow to a normal tempo.

I want you, Janice, her mind echoed. *I want you, Janice.*

She pressed trembling fingertips to her lips.

Was it true? Really true? A man like Taylor wanted to make love with *her?* Someone whose appearance was far from glamorous?

Yes, it was true, because she'd felt Taylor's arousal when she'd been nestled close to his body, seen the desire reflected in his eyes. It was true, because he'd walked away, having said the time wasn't right for them to take such a momentous, intimate step.

Dear heaven, how was this possible? she thought, shaking her head. Taylor was accepting her, wanting her, exactly as she was, without the sexy clothes, artfully applied makeup and wildly tumbling, seductive hair.

It was too much to comprehend all at once, she

thought, moving her fingers to her temples. It was so confusing, so new and unbelievable.

Because it had never happened before in her entire life.

Since she was a small child, her beauty had been everything, the measuring stick by which she was accepted or rejected.

True, Shirley was her friend with no questions asked, but that was far different from a man—from Taylor—seeing, wanting, the woman beneath the outer shell.

To her husband, even her own mother, she had been an object, a means to an end, that had resulted in the ultimate betrayal.

But now?

Now there was Taylor.

"Oh, God, this is so terribly complicated and confusing." Janice said aloud.

A wave of total exhaustion swept through her. She felt drained, so weary she could barely put one foot in front of the other. She locked the door, turned out the light and went to bed, falling immediately into a deep, dreamless sleep.

The next morning, Janice sat on her patio and watched the pair of hummingbirds enjoying the syrupy breakfast she'd provided for them. They hovered and sipped, staying close together, taking turns at the feeder in a ritual known only to them.

How strange, she thought as she drank her tea. She'd previously viewed the delicate birds as separate entities. Now she saw them as a couple, bonded for life, assured of the other's pleasure, as well as their own.

Janice sighed.

She felt so unsettled, as though everything in her well-ordered existence was suddenly topsy-turvy, not as it had been. So much had changed so quickly because of the emergence of Taylor in her life.

She set the cup and saucer on the table and wrapped her hands around her elbows in a protective gesture.

The walls she'd spent years constructing around herself were weakening, slowly but surely being chipped away by Taylor.

That was so dangerous, so foolish and wrong. If she allowed this to continue, she'd be exposed, vulnerable, with no defense against heartbreak.

She wanted to run as far away from Taylor as she could, as quickly as possible.

Janice sighed again.

No, that wasn't true. She wanted to stay, to be the recipient time and again of Taylor's kiss, touch, his smile. She wanted to see the passion in his eyes, hear him say how much he desired her. *Her.* Just as she was. Janice the woman, the person, not Janice the beautifully decorated doll.

"Enough of this," she said, getting to her feet. "I'm driving myself crazy."

An hour later, Janice was ready to leave the house to drive to Sleeping Beauty. She went in search of her glasses, finding them on the table in the living room where Taylor had placed them the night before. She picked them up, then hesitated.

It really had been a relief not to have the heavy frames pressing on her nose, she thought. Maybe they weren't really necessary. She had her hair in its usual tight bun, and she was wearing a navy-blue, oversize suit with navy Oxfords.

Yes? No? she thought, staring at the glasses.

"No," she said decisively.

She marched into the kitchen and tossed the glasses into the trash.

She wasn't making a fashion statement by disposing of the glasses, she decided. She was simply taking pity on her worn-out, tired nose. She wouldn't suddenly turn into a raving beauty because she no longer wore glasses.

In fact, she thought as she left the house, she doubted that anyone she encountered during the day would even notice that she wasn't wearing glasses.

"Thank you," Janice said, smiling.

The grandmother-type woman beamed at Janice. "No, dear, don't thank me. You should be thanking yourself for getting contact lenses instead of having to wear those heavy glasses. That was a lovely gift from you to you. Isn't that right, Ginger?"

"Oh, yes, Clara," her elderly companion said. "You have such pretty eyes, Janice. You'll enjoy looking at this funny old world we live in without having those cumbersome glasses in the way."

"I...I never thought of it quite like that before," Janice said. "A gift from me to me?"

"Absolutely," Ginger said. "We should enhance our personal attributes for ourselves. If those around us enjoy looking at what we've done, that's an added bonus." She laughed merrily. "My personal attributes are long since wrinkled and sagging, but in my day I was a beauty. Wasn't I, Clara?"

"You certainly were," Clara said. "But of more importance, you were my best friend. You were then, you are now. But, yes, indeed, you were stunning."

"And I enjoyed every minute of it," Ginger said. "I knew I was smashing, and when my Homer came into my life and appreciated what he saw, I knew he was an intelligent, sensitive man."

"But didn't you... What I mean is," Janice began, "didn't you wonder at times if Homer was attracted to your looks, instead of who you were as a person?"

"Heavens, no," Ginger said. "Because *I* knew who I was. Plus, Homer and I connected on all levels. The foundation of what we had wasn't based on our outer appearances. Do you understand, Janice?"

"I think so," Janice said, frowning.

"Anyway, dear," Ginger went on, "don't hide your lovely eyes behind those nasty glasses again. Enjoy the gifts that nature gave you."

"Ginger, look at the time," Clara said. "We were just going to pop in here for some lotion and be on our way. We're going to be late for tea with Homer and Franklin. Come along. Goodbye, Janice. We'll see you again soon.''

"Goodbye," she said. "And thank you.''

The two women left Sleeping Beauty and Janice wandered behind the counter, slipping onto the high stool she kept by the cash register. She propped her elbows on the counter and rested her chin in the palms of her hands.

Clara and Ginger were the sixteenth and seventeenth customers of the day and every one of them had complimented her on her eyes.

No one had gone further, suggesting she do something about her wardrobe or hairstyle. They'd simply commented on her pretty eyes.

It had been...well, nice. It was as though the women who had entered the store recognized something beautiful when they saw it and made a point of saying so. It had all been as simple, open and honest as that.

"And confusing," Janice said aloud.

Then Ginger had added another ingredient to the muddled pie—enhancing one's beauty for yourself, enjoying one's natural attributes.

If a woman connected on all levels with a man, then outer appearances were frosting on the cake.

There must be truth in Ginger's theory, Janice thought, because she and Homer were still together, well beyond the glamorous years of their youth.

How very different her mother's beliefs had been from those expressed by Ginger. All she'd ever heard as a child, then as a young woman was that beauty was everything, the only thing that mattered. Without it, she would have, would be, nothing of importance.

But today?

Today the people who had commented on her beautiful eyes had treated Janice with the same respect and friendliness they had when she'd worn the ugly glasses.

She'd established herself as the manager of Sleeping Beauty, a classy, well-run boutique, known for excellence of merchandise and service. That she decided to display her pretty eyes was worth acknowledging, but didn't change her relationship with the patrons of the shop.

"That's rather amazing," Janice said, frowning.

Did she have this straight? She wasn't the woman with beautiful eyes who ran Sleeping Beauty. She was the top-notch manager of Sleeping Beauty who happened to have beautiful eyes. Yes, that was apparently how the customers of her store viewed her.

"Amazing," she repeated, then smiled. "And wonderful."

Oh, my, she thought in the next instant. She was suddenly dealing with so many new things in her life. Taylor Sinclair had somehow opened a multitude of doors that were spilling forth an amalgam of data she was attempting to decipher all at the same time.

Taylor Sinclair.

He had not been far from her thoughts the entire day. And with his image in her mind's eye came the exquisite remembrance of the kisses shared with him, the heated passion that had consumed her, the want, the need, the heartfelt desire to make love with him in total abandon.

"Too much," Janice whispered. "It's just too much all at once."

Just slow down, stay calm, she told herself. She was still in control, doing fine. She could handle this, all of it, one thing at a time.

Couldn't she?

"Oh, stop thinking," she said, sliding off the stool. "Go fold a teddy."

That night Taylor telephoned Janice to remind her to bring a sweater along on the trip to Prescott. They'd ended up chatting for half an hour.

On Thursday evening he called to ask if she'd decided what samples of her merchandise she'd take to show Andrea and Brandon. They'd talked for an hour.

Friday night, Taylor phoned to confirm that he'd pick Janice up at ten the next morning. Two hours later she replaced the receiver with a soft smile on her lips.

She and Taylor never ran out of things to talk about, she thought as she prepared for bed. It was all just chit-chat, getting-to-know-you-better topics, with Taylor sharing hilarious stories of his youthful escapades in Prescott. He, along with Brandon

Hamilton and someone named Ben Rizzoli had been busy, mischievous little boys.

Janice got into bed and snapped off the light on the nightstand.

Well, tomorrow was the big day. She rolled onto her stomach, wiggling into a comfortable position.

In a handful of hours, she thought sleepily, she'd be on her way to Prescott.

With Taylor.

Taylor lay in bed, his hands linked beneath his head on the pillow as he smiled up at a ceiling he couldn't see in the darkness.

It had been a good week...no, correct that...a great week, and the high point of each day had been the conversations with Janice on the phone.

She had a terrific sense of humor and a quick, intelligent mind. She had definite opinions she didn't hesitate to express, but she was willing to listen to new ideas and viewpoints with an open attitude.

She'd skittered around answering any in-depth questions regarding her life before opening Sleeping Beauty, but she had urged him to tell more and more stories about his childhood in Prescott. Her lilting laughter in response to his tales had come through the telephone to flow over him in a warm cascade.

Oh, yes, it had been a great week.

And tomorrow? Hell, tomorrow was going to be fantastic. He'd pick up Janice at exactly ten o'clock and they'd be off, whizzing along the mountain highway for a weekend in Prescott…together.

Well, not together in the sense of spending the weekend together as he had with women in the past, but together all the same.

He was looking forward to it, more than he would be able to put into words if pressed to do so.

He was going to spend forty-eight hours in cool, pretty Prescott, Arizona.

With Janice.

Chapter Eight

Janice walked slowly across the lobby of Hamilton
House, her gaze sweeping over everything within
view. She stopped in the center of the large expanse
and turned to look at Taylor, her eyes sparkling.

"Oh, Taylor," she said, smiling, "this is absolutely beautiful. It's like stepping back in time."

Taylor chuckled. "I take it that you like it?"

"Like it? I love it. Every detail imaginable has
been thought of." She paused. "Where do Andrea
and Brandon intend to put the shops?"

"You can ask them yourself. They're about to
pounce on us."

Janice turned again to see a couple with welcoming smiles approaching them.

Brandon Hamilton was tall and well-built, his

dark suit accentuating his broad shoulders and long legs. He had black hair, dark eyes, and was ruggedly handsome.

Andrea Hamilton had delicate features and big, dark eyes. Her shiny, swinging hair was dark brown, worn in a smooth, blunt cut to just above her shoulders. She was wearing a calf-length, paisley print dress that nipped in at her tiny waist.

They were an attractive couple, looked...well, as though they belonged together.

A sudden image of the pair of hummingbirds on her patio flashed before Janice's eyes.

Two by two, she thought. That was how society was constructed. Pairs. A woman, a man. A female, a male. Even the hummingbirds knew that.

Where was this nonsense coming from? she admonished herself. Her thoughts echoed "oh-poor-me-I'm-all-alone." She was perfectly content with her single status, with her life exactly the way it was.

"Hello, hello," Andrea said as she and Brandon stopped in front of Janice and Taylor. "Welcome to Hamilton House. It's nice to see you again, Taylor. And you must be Janice Jennings."

Taylor made the official introductions. He watched Brandon's face, seeing his friend frown slightly as he greeted Janice.

Brandon's reaction to Janice was right on target, Taylor thought. Brandon was reaching the conclusion that Janice was very pretty...but then again...she wasn't.

Janice was wearing her typical boxy, too big suit, this one kelly-green. The clunky Oxfords of the day were off-white to match the high-necked blouse. Her hair was in the usual bun.

But there were no heavy glasses on Janice's nose, and he was taking credit for that. He'd refrained from mentioning the absence of the glasses during the drive up to Prescott.

Yep, Brandon was seeing Janice's beautiful face and dynamite eyes in all their splendor, but the entire package that was Janice was off kilter. And Brandon knew it.

"...along that wall," Andrea was saying to Janice.

Taylor tuned back into the conversation.

"The plans Taylor told me about sound wonderful," Janice said. "I can easily picture the cobblestone walkway, the lampposts, everything."

"We're very excited about the project," Brandon said, encircling Andrea's shoulders with one arm. "Have you two had lunch?"

"No," Taylor said "And we're ready to eat."

"Good," Andrea said. "We have a table reserved in the dining room." She paused and laughed. "No, I can't stand it. Will you faint dead away from hunger if we look at the samples Janice brought from Sleeping Beauty before we eat, Taylor? I'm so eager to see them."

"I'll grin and bear it," he said. "Just don't comment if my stomach growls. I'll go bring in our luggage and the boxes from Sleeping Beauty. They're in the car.''

"I'll go with you, Taylor," Brandon said.

"Janice and I will meet you two in the conference room," Andrea said.

Taylor and Brandon left the hotel and crossed the street to the designated parking lot. Taylor opened the trunk of his car.

"I don't get it," Brandon said, speaking for the first time since the two men had made their exit.

"Don't get what?" Taylor said.

"Janice," Brandon said. "That is one very beautiful woman, but..." He stopped speaking and shook his head.

"Yep," Taylor said, smiling. "She's beautiful, all right. Those eyes of hers could stop traffic."

"But why the awful clothes?" Brandon said. "And the spinster schoolteacher hairdo?"

"I don't know for sure why Janice dresses the way she does." Taylor shoved his hands into the pockets of the gray slacks he wore with a lightweight, white sweater. "I managed to get her to ditch a pair of thick, dark-framed glasses—glasses that did not have prescription lenses."

"She's intentionally downplaying her beauty?" Brandon said, raising his eyebrows.

"I think so," Taylor said, nodding. "I thought at first she might not know how gorgeous she is, but now I'm beginning to believe she's hiding her natural attributes."

"Weird," Brandon said, shaking his head.

"No, she's just very complicated." Taylor paused. "But you know something, Brandon? The more time I spend with Janice, talking, sharing, the less her appearance matters. I find myself not even thinking about it more often than not."

"Mmm," Brandon said.

"Janice is intelligent, a very savvy business-woman," Taylor went on. "She has a great sense of humor, is right on top of world events, sports, movies—hell, the whole nine yards.

"She... What is that fool grin on your face supposed to mean?"

"A tad fond of the complicated Ms. Jennings are you, old chum?" Brandon said, still grinning his fool grin.

"No. Well, yes, I...like her. What's not to like? She's intelligent and—"

"Cut," Brandon said, slicing one hand through the air. "Don't repeat the whole list, for Pete's sake. Well, this should be a very interesting weekend. Yep, very interesting."

"Put a cork in it, Hamilton." Taylor reached into the trunk, retrieved a stack of boxes and shoved them at Brandon. "Make yourself useful."

Brandon wrapped his arms around the boxes. "I already have. I was the one who told you that you might very well be lonely and not even realize it, remember? There is definitely something brewing between you and the mysterious Janice."

"You're pushing me, Hamilton," Taylor said, taking two suitcases from the trunk.

"I hope so," Brandon said, smiling. "You're overdue to be pushed." He glanced down at the logo on the boxes he held. "Sleeping Beauty. Know what I think?"

"No, but I'm sure you're going to tell me," Taylor said, glaring at him.

"I think the name Sleeping Beauty applies not only to Janice's boutique, but to the lady herself."

"What?"

"Think about it," Brandon said. "The question is whether or not you're the prince who will kiss awake the sleeping beauty. Oh, yeah, this is going to be quite a weekend. I wouldn't miss it for the world."

When the two men returned to the hotel, Andrea informed them that she'd realized that in her excitement to see the merchandise from Sleeping Beauty, she'd failed to recognize the fact that Janice might prefer to check into her room and freshen up.

Taylor was to go to the fifth floor to deliver Janice's suitcase to her. Brandon gave Taylor a key to Andrea and Brandon's apartment, which was on the same floor, telling him to leave his luggage in their spare bedroom.

They would all meet in the conference room in fifteen minutes.

"Yes, ma'am," Taylor said, smiling at Andrea. "Got it, ma'am. I'm off to do as instructed."

"All men should be so cooperative," Andrea said, sliding a look at Brandon, who winked at her.

"I promise I won't peek at the samples from Sleeping Beauty while we're waiting." She paused. "Well, maybe just a teeny little look."

"Nope," Brandon said, tightening his hold on the boxes he held. "Janice probably has a presentation all planned. You can't touch anything until she comes back downstairs, sweet wife."

"Well, darn it," Andrea said. "Taylor, your Janice is so nice. I feel so comfortable with her, as though I've known her forever."

"She isn't mine," Taylor said, frowning.

"Figure of speech," Andrea said. "Shoo. Go. Janice is waiting for her suitcase."

Taylor headed for the elevator on the far wall of the lobby.

"So, you like Janice?" Brandon said to Andrea once Taylor was out of earshot.

"Oh, very much. She's friendly, warm, just delightful. I can see why she'd have loyal customers. She's pleasant to be with."

"Didn't you find her appearance a bit unusual?" Brandon said, raising his eyebrows.

Andrea nodded slowly. "Yes, I did. Janice is beautiful, but she's doing everything possible not to be. She's a mystery in a way, a very complex person. Taylor has his work cut out for him."

"I happen to agree with you, but what makes you think that Taylor is interested in Janice beyond just being her accountant?"

"Brandon, Brandon, Brandon," Andrea said. "I'm a woman. I know these things by instinct.

You just watch. The aunts will pick up on it in a flash.''

"Hey, I wouldn't dream of arguing the point," he said, "even if I didn't believe that you're right on the money. The female mind is far beyond my comprehension."

"Of course it is, sweetheart," Andrea said, smiling at him warmly. "Let's take those boxes into the conference room. Oh, this is so exciting. I can hardly wait to see the goodies from Sleeping Beauty."

"Taylor needs to discover a great deal more about Sleeping Beauty than just what's in these boxes," Brandon said.

"What?" she said, obviously confused.

Brandon leaned over the stack of boxes in his arms and dropped a quick kiss on Andrea's lips.

"Andrea, my love," he said. "Don't attempt to understand the genius-level workings of the male mind. You'll become frustrated when faced with continual defeat."

Andrea rolled her eyes heavenward, then started off toward the designated room.

Janice was smiling when she answered Taylor's knock at the door.

"Suitcase delivery," he said, matching her smile.

"Thank you. Do come in." She stepped back to allow him to enter. "Oh, Taylor, look at this room." She closed the door and swept one arm through the air. "Isn't it exquisite? I think if I look out the window, I'll see horses and buggies on the street instead of cars. The decorating in here is picture-perfect turn of the century.''

"Yep," Taylor said, placing her suitcase on the bed. He set his own luggage on the floor. "Brandon did a helluva fine job when he restored Hamilton House and..." He stopped speaking when he saw Janice staring at his suitcase. "Problem?"

"Why is that in my room?" she said, pointing at his suitcase.

"It's mine," he said.

"I realize that, Taylor."

"It's mine and, therefore, it belongs with me, where I am. You know what I mean?"

Janice narrowed her eyes as she looked at Taylor intently.

She could see the flicker of merriment in Taylor's dark eyes. He was stringing her along, just to determine what kind of reaction he would get. At the moment, he was behaving like the mischievous little boy he'd been while growing up here in Prescott.

Well, sit tight, Sinclair. She could give as good as she got. Tit for tat.

"Problem?" she said with an expression of pure innocence. "That has yet to be determined. It all depends on one very crucial issue."

Taylor frowned. "It does?"

"Oh, my, yes. It's a biggy, all right, could be a major stumbling block." She paused. "We might as well get it over with and hope for the best."

"Huh?"

Janice closed the distance between them and encircled Taylor's neck with her arms.

"Taylor," she said, her voice a husky whisper. "Do you—" she batted her eyelashes. "—do you…snore?"

Taylor stiffened in shock, then a moment later heard the tiny giggle that escaped from Janice's lips. He burst into laughter, pulled her arms from his neck, and kissed each of her hands before releasing them.

"Score one for you, Ms. Jennings," he said. "You had me going there for a second."

"You deserved it."

"I know," he said, laughing again. "I will now go deposit my suitcase in Andrea and Brandon's apartment and return to collect you, madam. Farewell."

"Ta-ta."

After Taylor grabbed his suitcase and left the room, Janice's smile faded as she shifted her gaze to the four-poster bed.

She and Taylor had been joking regarding whether they were to share that pretty, old-fashioned bed.

But she knew that deep within her, the want, the desire to make love with Taylor was there, simmering, glowing like embers waiting to be fanned into licking flames that she would allow to consume her.

Oh, yes, she did wish to make love with Taylor Sinclair.

With a sigh, Janice opened her suitcase and began to hang her clothes in the closet.

Taylor, Taylor, Taylor, her mind hummed. For now, at least, he was accepting her just as she was. How wondrous that was. What a special gift he was giving her.

It wouldn't last, she knew, because Taylor was accustomed to keeping company with beautiful women.

But what if…what if…while she was the center of his attention, while he actually wanted to make love with her, she lowered her protective walls and created cherished memories with Taylor that would be hers to keep?

What if she made love with Taylor Sinclair?

Janice placed her cosmetic bag in the bathroom, knowing there was no makeup in it—no eye shadow, mascara, blush or lipstick. There were simply a brush and comb, light lotion and tissues. Nothing to enhance her features. Nothing to turn her into more than being just Janice, who Taylor actually, unbelievably desired.

After putting her lingerie from Sleeping Beauty in the dresser drawers, she set the empty suitcase in the closet, then settled onto the side of the bed to wait for Taylor's return.

There was no way she could be emotionally hurt by taking the momentous, intimate step with Taylor. She wouldn't fall *in* love with the man—heavens no—she simply wanted to *make* love with him.

She realized what she and Taylor had together was temporary, would be over very quickly, just as soon as Taylor grew weary of being with a woman who didn't evoke the envy of other men when they walked into a room. He wouldn't settle for a woman like her for long, because he didn't have to.

So, it was now, or it was never.

"Well, Janice?" she said aloud. "Just how far does your 'I can handle this' attitude go?"

Before she could search her heart and mind for an answer to the so-very-important question, a knock sounded at the door. Janice got to her feet and crossed the room to open the door for Taylor.

A little over an hour later, Janice and Taylor, Andrea and Brandon were seated at a table in the dining room of Hamilton House, having just had crisp salads placed in front of them.

"I remember food," Taylor said. "Even though it has been an eternity since I had any."

"Poor baby," Andrea said, laughing. "Do you want my salad, too, Taylor? Or is one enough?"

"I'll hold myself back," he said, "because I know I have a steak sandwich with my name on it being prepared in the kitchen."

"You're a brave soul," Andrea said, patting his hand.

Brandon lifted his water glass. "A toast to Janice and her Sleeping Beauty boutique. The newest member of the shops to be built in Hamilton House.''

"Hear, hear," Taylor said, raising his glass.

The four clinked their glasses together.

"It's so exciting," Andrea said after they'd taken an official sip of water. "Your merchandise is exquisite, Janice."

"And expensive," Brandon said, cocking one eyebrow at his wife. "A fact I'm well aware of since you purchased half of Janice's samples."

"Well, goodness, Brandon," Andrea said, smiling. "They were my size, were meant to be mine. Besides, how can I recommend the products in our specialty shops with a clear conscience if I haven't tested them?" She looked at Janice. "Right, Janice? You wear items from Sleeping Beauty, don't you?"

Taylor's head snapped around and he stared at Janice intently.

Uh-oh, he thought. Andrea was treading on dangerous ground. A woman who dressed like Janice didn't wear sexy lingerie. Cripe, what was Andrea thinking? Couldn't she tell that Janice was a white-cotton undies type?

"Well, I..." Janice said.

"Pass the salt," Taylor interjected. "Please."

Brandon handed him the salt shaker that Taylor could have reached easily on his own.

"I..." Janice started again.

"And the pepper," Taylor said.

"Is your arm broken?" Brandon said, smacking the pepper shaker into Taylor's hand.

"Do you need anything else, Taylor?" Janice said.

"No," he said, then turned to Andrea. "I imagine it would be like working in an ice cream store. People who work in ice cream stores reach a point where they can't stand the sight of ice cream. Nope. Can't stand the stuff. They never take a lick from a cone, or a bite from a bowl. Get it? Therefore, Janice wouldn't wear the merchandise from Sleeping Beauty because—"

"Excuse me, Taylor," Janice interrupted, "but you're wrong. To answer your question, Andrea, yes, I have a complete wardrobe of Sleeping Beauty merchandise, as well as the lotions, bath beads, and other accessories."

"You do?" Taylor said, his eyes widening as he stared at her.

"I certainly do," she said, lifting her chin and meeting his startled gaze directly. "Words can't describe how sensuous, how feminine it feels to have satin and lace caressing one's skin. It's heavenly."

"Oh," Taylor managed to say as heat rocketed through his body.

Janice laughed. "Well, this is a first. I'm sitting here discussing my underclothes."

"I hope I like my tap pants," Andrea said. "I've never owned a pair."

"I'm wearing tap pants with a matching camisole right now," Janice said. "They're extremely comfortable. I'm sure you'll enjoy the set you purchased from the samples I brought. They'll glide over your skin with a gentle touch as you move like...like a feathery kiss.''

Good Lord, Taylor thought, shifting in his chair, he was dying right there on the spot. Janice actually wore lingerie from Sleeping Beauty? Unbelievable. And the way she was describing it was causing him to go up in flames.

Would this woman never stop surprising him? Never cease to reveal another layer of herself that he hadn't known existed?

"Problem, buddy?" Brandon said, grinning as he looked at Taylor.

"Shut up, Hamilton," Taylor said, glaring at him.

Brandon shrugged. "Just thought I'd ask."

"No wonder your boutique is so successful, Janice," Andrea said, ignoring the interchange between the men. "No woman could resist purchasing your merchandize once you've described it the way you just did.

"We must be certain that the manager of the Sleeping Beauty shop here in Hamilton House can express herself as well as you do."

"I give all my employees a variety of apparel free of charge when I hire them," Janice said. "It's a sound investment, because once they wear the items their enthusiasm is contagious. The mental images they evoke in potential customers is very vivid."

"No joke," Taylor muttered.

Brandon heard him and burst into laughter.

"Did we miss something?" Andrea said, looking at Brandon questioningly.

"Food," Taylor said as the waitress appeared, carrying a large tray. "That's what's missing here...food."

"You certainly act strangely when you aren't fed on a regular basis, Taylor," Janice said.

"I know," he said. "Ignore me. I've been like this ever since I was a little kid. You can ask my dad. He'll tell you that I need my nourishment or I get weird, very weird."

Brandon fell apart laughing, prompting Andrea to thump him on the back when his hilarity resulted in a coughing fit.

To Taylor's utmost relief the conversation shifted to other topics while the four consumed the delicious meal.

Hours later, Janice slipped a burnt-orange, long-sleeved caftan over her head and waited for it to settle into place at mid-calf.

"An orange tent," she said, peering down at the abundance of material.

She'd replaced the sturdy Oxfords with simple, bone-colored two-inch heels, but her hair remained in the severe bun.

She sank onto the edge of the bed and yawned.

Her kingdom for a nap, she thought. During the pleasant afternoon she'd spent with Taylor exploring Prescott, she'd yawned several times, causing Taylor to chuckle. It was the altitude getting to her, he'd explained.

It had been such a fun outing amd she'd met a multitude of friendly people who Taylor had known all his life.

Janice blinked several times, then yawned again, patting her hand against her mouth. "Goodness, I'm so sleepy."

She got to her feet and walked around the room, hoping to dispel the need to curl up on the bed and give way to the sleepy state that was creeping steadily over her.

Wake up, she ordered herself. She wasn't going to be sparkling company at dinner if she didn't escape from this fog. Andrea and Brandon had planned a gathering that was to include Brandon's great-aunts Prudence and Charity, plus Dr. Ben Rizzoli, the boyhood friend of both Brandon and Taylor's.

Janice's glance fell on a pretty box she'd set on the top of the dresser.

She was so pleased with the purchase she'd made. The pair of crystal hummingbirds mounted on a wooden stand would be lovely on the mantel above the fireplace in her living room.

And every time she looked at the delicate statue she would, she knew, have a rush of memories of this special weekend.

Janice smiled as she replayed the hours of the afternoon in her mind.

How fortunate Taylor was, and Brandon, too, to have grown up in this warm and welcoming little town. What happy childhood years they'd both had.

She frowned.

No, she wasn't going to take the road that would lead to dwelling on her own youth. There was nothing to be gained from that except dimming her euphoric, albeit sleepy, state of mind. She'd concentrate on the carefree hours she'd spent with Taylor.

Not once during their tour of Prescott had Taylor explained that Janice was a client of his. He'd introduced her time and again as "My friend, Janice Jennings, from Phoenix," often slipping one arm around her shoulders in the process.

Typical small-town gossip must be humming, she thought, as Taylor had given every indication to those he spoke with that he and Janice were together, really together, for a weekend stay at Hamilton House.

Why had he done that? If she was a stunning beauty, she could understand it. Let the hometown folks see what handsome, worldly Taylor Sinclair was accustomed to having on his arm.

But to show off her? That didn't make one bit of sense.

"Will I ever figure that man out?" she said, throwing up her hands. "I seriously doubt it."

Janice glanced at her watch, then the door, expecting Taylor's knock at any moment.

Taylor stood in the hallway outside Janice's door, his hands in his pockets, a frown on his face.

He'd rushed through his shower, tossed on slacks and a sweater, and nearly sprinted down the hall from Andrea and Brandon's apartment to Janice's room.

He'd only left her an hour or so before, yet there he was, acting like an overeager adolescent who was anticipating the moment when he would see Janice again.

Man, oh, man, he'd enjoyed the hours that he'd spent with Janice. Her eyes had sparkled with excitement at all the new things she was seeing, and her smile had been genuine when she met people who were important to him.

He'd been...well, proud to introduce Ms. Janice Jennings to those he'd known all his life. Yes, proud. Janice was the real goods—open, friendly, honest. He hadn't given a moment's thought to the way she was dressed, as he presented Janice, the person, to his friends.

And he'd felt ten feet tall.

Taylor narrowed his eyes and stared at the door.

Face it, he thought. He was a mental mess. Janice was confusing him so completely, it was a crime.

His feelings for her were growing steadily. He cared for her. He truly cared for her, very, very much.

And heaven knew he desired her, wanted to make love with her with an intensity beyond anything he'd experienced before.

Why? Damn it, why?

Janice was opposite—and then some—from the

women he kept company with. She didn't fit the mold, not even close. But for reasons he couldn't begin to explain she was getting to him...big time.

Why? That was question number one. And question two? What was he going to do about it?

"Hey, hotshot," a voice said. "Are you having a conversation with that door? Does it have anything interesting to say?"

Taylor turned in the direction of the voice, and instantly smiled.

"Hi there, Aunt Charity," he said. "Good evening, Aunt Prudence." He rapped quickly on Janice's door. "It's great to see you again."

Janice opened the door.

"And this is Janice Jennings," Taylor went on. "Janice, these two wonderful ladies are the loves of my life. May I present Aunt Prudence and Aunt Charity?"

Janice smiled in delight. "Hello. I've heard so much about you, and I've been looking forward to meeting you both."

The elderly women were the same height and had identical features, befitting twins. Aunt Prudence was wearing a navy-blue, high-necked old fashioned dress. Aunt Charity was decked out in a bright pink taffeta creation that reminded Janice of something that might have been worn in a turn of the century dance hall.

"The pleasure is ours, dear," Aunt Prudence said.

"You bet, honey," Aunt Charity said. "It's

about time that Taylor brought a gal home for us to meet.''

"Oh, I'm not..." Janice started.

"Sure you are," Charity said. "Let's go eat. I'm hungry."

Janice hurried to retrieve her purse, then stepped out into the hall, closing the door behind her.

"I understand you're going to have one of the new shops in the lobby, Janice," Aunt Prudence said as the four walked toward the elevator.

"It's called Sleeping Beauty," Charity said. "Sells fancy undies."

Janice laughed, deciding she already adored the notorious aunts.

Fancy undies, Taylor mentally repeated, his gaze sweeping over Janice's billowing, shapeless dress. After that killer conversation at lunch, he now knew that beneath that awful orange thing that Janice was wearing was sensuous, satin and lace lingerie from Sleeping Beauty.

That thought niggling at him for the entire evening just might be enough to push him right over the edge of his sanity.

"Are you enjoying your visit to Prescott, dear?" Aunt Pru said to Janice as the group entered the elevator.

"Oh, yes," Janice said, "I'm having a wonderful time. Everything is...well, perfect."

"It is?" Taylor said.

Janice smiled at him warmly. "It is."

Now he felt *twenty* feet tall, Taylor thought, unable to curb his smile.

"Way to go, big boy," Aunt Charity said, poking Taylor in the ribs with her elbow.

Taylor laughed, but sobered in the next instant.

Way to go? he thought. He sure wished he knew just where he and Janice were actually going in this strange relationship of theirs.

He needed answers.

And he fully intended to get them.

Soon.

Chapter Nine

Taylor straightened a bright red sweater over the jeans he was wearing to Andrea and Brandon's wedding reception on the town square that afternoon. He combed his hair, glanced at his watch...again...then slouched onto an easy chair in Andrea and Brandon's apartment.

It was still too early to collect Janice and walk over to the square for the party, he thought. And there he was again, acting like an ants-in-his-pants teenager waiting to pick up his date.

Taylor rested his elbows on the arms of the chair, made a steeple of his fingers and tapped his lips restlessly against them.

Dinner the previous night had been a really enjoyable event, he mused. He'd had a terrific time, pure and simple. Everyone liked Janice, he could tell, and it was obvious that her warmth and openness were genuine.

Ben Rizzoli had been his usual charming self, although he had seemed a bit preoccupied at times. Aunt Pru had frowned with concern whenever she'd looked in Ben's direction.

Just what he needed. Another mystery. More unanswered questions. Maybe he'd get an opportunity to speak with Ben alone during the reception.

Taylor checked his watch again, then shook his head in self-disgust.

He'd urged Janice to sleep late since she was obviously suffering from the effect of the mile-high altitude. He'd spent the morning with Brandon, lugging cases of soda to the plaza and putting the cans in tubs of ice. The activity had served as only a minor distraction.

So, Janice? Taylor thought. How are you? What frame of mind are you in today, lovely lady? What will you choose to wear to a picnic on the square to cover up your sexy, Sleeping Beauty lingerie?

Sleeping Beauty. Yes, Brandon was right. That was exactly who Janice Jennings was…Sleeping Beauty.

She was waiting for her prince, the man who would awaken her, give her the confidence to emerge from her cocoon and become the beautiful butterfly she was capable of being.

A man who loved her enough to encourage her to embrace the full extent of her femininity.

Love Janice? Fall in love, be in love, with Janice Jennings? Lord, that was a terrifying thought. To love was to eventually lose, to suffer heartache beyond measure.

Love came, then was gone, either through death or a disintegration of that love from the pressures of day-to-day life.

No, thank you, he'd pass.

But what if he fell in love with Janice despite his fierce determination not to? Could that actually happen? Hell, he didn't know.

What he did know was that leaving Janice at her door last night after sharing a searing kiss with her had been one of the most difficult things he'd ever done. She'd responded to that kiss totally, had seemed to melt into him, become a part of him, that he definitely had not wanted to let go.

This wasn't the time, he'd mumbled to Janice. Andrea and Brandon were expecting him to sleep in their guest room. When they made love, it would be private, theirs, not common knowledge to everyone around them.

"When," Taylor said.

He kept saying that. Not *if,* but *when,* and Janice never called him on the carpet about that choice of a word. She wanted him, desired him, wished to make love with him with the same intensity that he wanted her.

But what if *making* love with Janice pushed him over the emotional edge, caused him to fall *in* love with her?

"No," Taylor said, lunging to his feet.

He began to pace, hands shoved into his pockets, a deep frown on his face.

He had to back off, to put some distance between himself and Janice, return to his original role of being her accountant, nothing more. To continue on the path he was heading with Janice was far too emotionally dangerous.

Taylor stopped in his tracks as a chill swept through him.

That would mean he would never kiss Janice again, never hold her in his arms, nestle her close to his body, never see her expressive blue eyes turn smoky with want, desire for him, only him.

Lord, what a cold, empty picture that painted in his beleaguered mind.

You could be lonely even as we speak and not even know it.

"Okay, okay," Taylor said, resuming his trek around the room.

Janice had filled a void within him that he hadn't realized existed, he admitted to himself. He felt...complete when he was with her.

He wanted to stay by her side, missed her when they were separated even for a short length of time, was acutely aware of his masculinity when Janice, the woman, was with him.

Janice's smile was like a precious gift, her lilting laughter like music. The sparkle in her eyes was more beautiful than the most expensive sapphires. Her honesty and innocence—her *realness*—were so rare, so wonderful, they were meant to be cherished.

The image in his mind of a future without Janice was so bleak, and dark, and empty. She was sunshine and flowers, a breath of fresh, spring air.

She was his.

And this, Taylor thought frantically, must be love.

He stopped again and dragged shaking hands down his face.

"Oh, Lord," he said, looking up at the ceiling. "What have I gone and done? And what in the hell am I going to do about it?"

Run, his mind hammered. He had to put physical and emotional distance between himself and Janice. *Now.* He would not, could not, touch her again, nor hold or kiss her. No.

Love not nurtured would dim, flicker like the flame on a candle, then finally disappear, just cease to exist. He would regain command of his heart, his mind and soul, wouldn't be rendered vulnerable, without protection against the agony of heartache that came when love ended.

But...

The mere thought of walking out of Janice's life was already causing him pain. His heart hurt, it actually, physically hurt.

Now wait a minute. He was in charge. He was making the conscious decision to end his relationship with Janice. Surely that pain would ebb quicker than if he allowed fate to call the shots.

Wouldn't it?

"Ah, hell," he said fiercely. "I'm a wreck, a total wreck."

He had to calm down, get a grip. He couldn't think all this through clearly because he was about to spend more time with Janice.

They'd attend the wedding reception together, then they still had the drive back down the mountain to get through.

His thoughts would simply have to go on hold until he was safely in his own apartment in Phoenix, alone, able to view the situation reasonably and rationally.

In the meantime, he'd blank his mind, force a smile and survive the remainder of this day. Somehow.

In her room, Janice began to twist her hair into its usual bun, then hesitated.

A bun for a picnic? she thought. Maybe that was a bit much. She was wearing baggy tan slacks and a shapeless green tunic that hung to the middle of her thighs.

Perhaps her apparel was enough camouflage for this particular event. She could afford to give an inch. She didn't wish to totally embarrass Taylor by her appearance.

"Fine," she said, nodding decisively. "One teeny, tiny inch."

She twisted her hair into the single braid that she wore when she went swimming in her pool. After securing the end with a rubber band she found in her cosmetic bag, she peeked at her reflection in the mirror.

So much for her grand concession, she thought. She didn't look any different from before. Wearing a braid down her back, instead of a bun at the nape of her neck, was not a major happening, except that it was much more comfortable not to have that bulky weight on her neck. It reminded her of no longer suffering from tired-nose syndrome from the unnecessary glasses.

"Taylor probably won't even notice my hair," she said aloud with a shrug.

Taylor most definitely noticed.

When Janice answered his knock at the door, she greeted him with a cheerful hello, then spun around to hurry to the bed to retrieve her purse.

Taylor's eyes widened and his heart began to beat a wild tattoo as he saw the long, golden braid swing through the air.

Lord, he thought, Janice's glorious hair was that long? Imagine, just imagine, what it would be like falling free when they made love, caressing his body with a silken touch, cascading over Janice's breasts in a tantalizing curtain to be brushed aside by him to glimpse the feminine bounty beneath.

Janice Jennings was torturing him, killing him by inches, right there on the spot.

"I'm all set," Janice said, returning to stand in front of Taylor, a bright smile on her face. "Do you know that this is the very first picnic I've ever been on in my entire life?''

This woman had stolen his heart, Taylor thought incredulously. She'd actually done it. There was no denying it, nowhere to hide from the truth.

He was deeply in love with Janice.

"Taylor?" Janice cocked her head slightly to one side and looked at him questioningly. "Is something wrong? You're awfully pale all of a sudden. Are you ill?''

Ill? Taylor thought. Yeah, he was ill, if being insane counted. Falling in love was the last thing he'd intended to do in his lifetime. He was so damn angry with himself, he could spit.

"Taylor?"

"What? Oh, I'm sorry. I was off in space somewhere.'' He cleared his throat when he heard the raspy quality of his voice. "I...I like your hair that way, Janice.''

"You do?" She caught the braid and pulled it to the front of her body. "I didn't think you'd even notice. When I looked in the mirror, I couldn't see any difference in my appearance.''

Taylor dragged his gaze from where the braid was sloped sensuously over Janice's right breast, and looked directly into her eyes.

"There's a difference," he said, nodding. "Your hair is...I don't know...softer around your face. It's very nice, attractive, very pretty. You sure have a lot of hair, don't you? It's lovely...your hair. It's like a marigold, a..." He paused and shook his head. "Ah, hell, forget it."

"A marigold? Why thank you, Taylor. That's a compliment I'll cherish. You continually...well, you make me feel very special."

Because I'm in love with you, damn it, Taylor's mind hollered. *And guess what, Janice Jennings? That really ticks me off.*

"Come on," he said gruffly. "We're going to be late to the party."

As Janice and Taylor walked toward the square, she slid glances at him, noting the tight set to his jaw, the frown lines etched between his eyebrows.

Why was Taylor so grumpy? she wondered. There was obviously something troubling him that had caused him to be in a less-than-chipper mood. But even cranky he was so handsome, so virile, just oozed a blatant masculinity that was nearly tangible.

She wanted to step in front of him, forcing him to stop, then wrap her arms around his neck and kiss him until they were both dizzy with desire.

Shame on you, she thought, swallowing a bubble of laughter that threatened to escape from her lips. But, oh, goodness, she felt so happy, young, carefree. She was about to take part in her very first picnic with the most magnificent man she'd ever known.

Taylor, who made her feel so feminine, a perfect counterpart to his masculinity.

Taylor, who accepted her just as she was, which was a gift to her that was so rare and wonderful it defied description in its splendor.

Taylor, who inch by emotional inch was chipping away at her protective walls, coming closer and closer to capturing her heart for all time.

Oh, my, she thought, nearly stumbling. Was she falling in love with Taylor Sinclair?

"Why haven't you ever been on a picnic?" Taylor said suddenly, drawing Janice from her shocking thoughts.

"What? Oh, well, my mother wasn't into things like picnics. She had a one-track mind."

"Set on what?" he said, glancing over at her.

Beauty pageants, Janice thought. Parading her daughter in front of judges, strangers, the people who would determine if she was beautiful enough to pass, to be accepted, the one to win the prize. Damnable beauty pageants.

"It's not important," she said. "It was a very long time ago. Old news. My goodness, look at all the people on the square. This is going to be quite a party."

"Mmm," Taylor said.

What was Janice keeping from him? he thought. Whenever the subject of her youth, her mother, came up, she skittered in another direction.

Didn't she trust him enough to share her innermost secrets with him?

What was it about her childhood, her mother, that upset her? What had caused the pain he'd seen in her beautiful blue eyes? He wanted, needed, to know, to be assured that Janice knew that he would never hurt her.

Their relationship was based on a foundation of honesty, of—

Oh, yeah?

If he was being so almighty honest with Janice, why didn't he open his mouth and declare his love for her? He was keeping a secret from her…big time.

I love you, Janice. Janice, I love you. In love with you, Janice, is what I am.

A trickle of sweat ran down Taylor's chest.

No way. He wasn't about to tell her how he felt. He was having enough trouble coming to grips with the realization of his emotions without blurting them for Janice to hear.

Besides, there was no point in telling her because he was determined to fall *out* of love with her. To love, to lose, to be ripped to shreds—no, it was more than he could handle.

As Janice and Taylor stepped onto the lush, grassy carpet of the square, the crackling excitement cascaded over them, along with a high volume of chatter and laughter. Blankets were spread everywhere as well as a generous number of lawn chairs.

"Hey, big boy," Aunt Charity yelled above the din. "We're over here."

Taylor smiled and waved, then he and Janice

wove their way through the crowd. Aunt Charity and Aunt Prudence were sitting on lawn chairs next to two blankets on the ground. A large wicker hamper was in the center of the blankets.

An attractive woman in her early thirties smiled the moment she saw Taylor, and rushed over to give him a hug.

"Hello, handsome man," she said. "It's wonderful to see you."

"Hello, sweetheart," Taylor said. "You're even more beautiful than the last time I saw you."

A knot tightened in Janice's stomach as she swept her gaze over the woman Taylor was holding in his arms.

She really was beautiful, she thought. She was tall and slender, had lovely green eyes and wavy, strawberry-blond hair that skimmed her shoulders. She was wearing snug jeans and a green sport top that accentuated her eyes and figure to perfection.

This was the type of woman Taylor was accustomed to being with. She was gorgeous and certainly self-assured, as evidenced by the way she'd flung her arms around Taylor without a second's hesitation.

Well, fine, Janice thought, taking a shaky breath. It was probably for the best that this had happened. It was a reality check, a reminder of the way things actually were.

The woman stepped out of Taylor's embrace and extended one hand to Janice.

"You must be Janice Jennings," she said, smiling. "I'm Jennifer Mackane. I'm the manager of the dining room at Hamilton House, but I've been enjoying my blissful days off while you've been staying at the hotel. I understand you're to have one of the specialty shops when they're up and running."

"Yes, that's right," Janice said, managing to produce a small smile as she shook Jennifer's hand. "It's a pleasure to meet you, Jennifer."

"We all owe you a thank-you for getting our Taylor up to Prescott again," Jennifer said. "I've missed him."

"Oh," Janice said.

"Taylor, Brandon and Ben—have you met Ben?" Jennifer went on. "Anyway, the three of them were like my big brothers when we all grew up here in Prescott. That was fine when we were little kids, but when I started dating I could have strangled them. They kept appearing at all the wrong moments, and wreaked complete havoc with my adolescent love life."

"Oh?" Janice repeated, a genuine smile lighting up her face.

"We took our roles as your big brothers very seriously," Taylor said, chuckling. "We still do, as a matter of fact. Are you dating anyone who needs to have the rules and regulations explained to him?"

Taylor viewed beautiful Jennifer Mackane as a sister? Janice's heart sang. Wasn't that just the sweetest thing?

"No, I am not," Jennifer said. "But I wouldn't tell you if I was, you troublemaker. There's only one guy in my life and he's all I need." She glanced around. "Oops. Where did he go?"

"There he is," Taylor said. "He's getting a ride on Brandon's shoulders, and they're headed this way."

Janice watched Brandon and Andrea approach. Perched on Brandon's shoulders was a cute little boy about four years old, who had the same color eyes and hair as Jennifer.

"Greetings," Brandon said, stopping by the group.

"Hi, Joey," Taylor said to the child. "I bet you can see everything from up there."

"Yep," Joey said. "I'm high as the sky, Uncle Taylor. I'm big, big, big."

"And heavy, heavy, heavy," Brandon said, swinging Joey to the ground. "What do you feed this kid, Jennifer?"

"I'm hungry, Mommy," Joey said.

Brandon laughed. "I rest my case."

"I'm four," Joey said to Janice, holding up the appropriate number of fingers. "I was three, but then I had my birthday party, and then I got to be four, so I'm four. Four is better than three."

"It certainly is," Janice said, smiling.

Oh, what a precious little boy, she thought. How blessed Jennifer Mackane was to have him. From the conversation that had taken place, it was obvious that Jennifer was a single mother, who was devoted to her son. Imagine seeing that cherub's face the first thing each morning, then tucking him safely into bed at night.

For heaven's sake, where was this maternal yearning coming from? She'd accepted the fact years before that she would never be a mother. But, oh, look at that face, that smile, that darling little boy.

"Do you play hopscotch, Joey?" she heard herself ask.

"No, no, no," he said, frowning. "That's a girl game. I'm a spaceship captain."

"This week," Jennifer said, laughing. "Last week he was a fire fighter. Come on, Joey, I want to say hello to Aunt Martha."

"'Kay." Joey grabbed Jennifer's hand, then began to hop forward on both feet. "I'm Tigger."

"We'll be back," Jennifer said over her shoulder. "Let's go, Tigger."

"What a wonderful child," Janice said, unable to suppress the wistful tone in her voice.

"Isn't he, though?" Andrea said.

"Want a couple of kids like Joey?" Brandon said, smiling at Andrea.

"Yes, I do," Andrea said, matching his smile. "Shall I place my order?"

"It's duly noted," Brandon said.

"Jennifer still isn't seeing anyone, Brandon?" Taylor said.

"No. She's very stubborn on the subject," Brandon said, frowning. "She says Joey is all she needs in her life. Janice, Jennifer's husband was killed in a construction accident a week before Joey was born."

"Oh, that's terrible," Janice said.

"Yeah, it was rough," Brandon said. "She hasn't dated anyone since Joe died."

"We're working on that," Aunt Charity said. "Where's Ben today by the way?"

"He's at the hospital," Brandon said. "There's a baby insisting on being born right in the middle of our wedding reception."

"How rude," Aunt Charity said. "Well, he may show up later."

"Does Ben seem sort of...I don't know... preoccupied or something to any of you?" Taylor said.

"Yes, dear," Aunt Prudence said with a sigh. "We're quite concerned about our Ben. There is definitely something troubling him."

"Mmm," Taylor said, frowning.

A family, Janice thought. All of these special people were like a big, warm, loving family. Did they realize how fortunate they were?

"Better get used to this," Taylor said, turning to smile at Janice. "You'll be coming up to check on the Sleeping Beauty outlet at Hamilton House quite often, I imagine. You'll be getting the latest news about everyone whether you're interested or not."

"Of course she'll be interested," Aunt Charity said. "Janice is a member of the family now."

Taylor reached behind Janice and pulled her long

braid forward, stroking the silken hair gently with his thumb.

"Yes," he said quietly, looking directly into Janice's eyes. "She is. She's a member of the family."

Chapter Ten

During the first hour of the drive down the mountain from Prescott, Janice chattered happily about the marvelous time she'd had at the picnic on the town square.

She raved about the wonderful, friendly people she'd met, how touching the toast that the mayor had made to Andrea and Brandon had been, the delicious food that had been discovered in the wicker hamper, and on and on.

When she finally floated off her cloud, she realized that Taylor was replying in monosyllables and not actually taking part in the conversation.

He mumbled something about not having had an opportunity to speak privately with Ben when his friend had finally arrived at the party, then fell silent again.

Janice looked over at Taylor, deciding not to press the issue of his rather solemn mood for fear that her own euphoric state of mind might be diminished.

Nothing was going to tarnish the memories of the weekend, she decided firmly. She'd had such fun, had felt so free, young and *accepted.* It had been glorious, all of it, and she'd treasure the remembrances of every hour.

She directed her attention to the beautiful sunset streaking across the heavens as they approached the edge of Phoenix.

One more try, she thought. She had no idea why Taylor was so quiet, seemed so distant, self-absorbed, but she'd make a last attempt to communicate with him.

"Isn't the sunset gorgeous, Taylor?" she said, breaking the oppressive silence in the car.

"What?" he said. "Oh, yes, nice, very pretty. Nothing can match an Arizona sunset."

"Taylor?" Janice turned toward him as much as her seatbelt would allow. "Is something wrong?"

"No," he said quickly. "I just have a great deal on my mind."

"Do you want to share? Talk about it? I'd listen, you know."

Share? Taylor mentally repeated. Share the fact that he was in love with her? Tell Janice the depth of his true and *honest* feelings for her? Announce that he was so terrified of that love that he had a cold fist tightened painfully in his gut?

"No. Thank you, but no," he said, producing a small smile. "I just have something on my mind that I have to work through."

Like how to fall *out* of love with Janice Jennings, he thought dismally.

"Fair enough," Janice said, nodding. "Well, I do want to thank you for a fabulous weekend."

"I'm glad you enjoyed yourself. You made a lot of new friends in Prescott, Janice. Everyone liked you very much. Whenever you drive up to check on the Sleeping Beauty store in Hamilton House, you'll be…well, welcomed home."

"As part of the family," she said softly.

Taylor reached across the console and squeezed one of her hands gently.

"Yes," he said. "You're now a member of the family up there."

He released her hand and gripped the steering wheel again.

Janice stared at him for a long moment, took a steadying breath, then lifted her chin.

"And here, Taylor?" she said. "In this car? Who am I here, right now, with you?"

The woman I love, he thought. She was his, in his heart, mind and soul, and he couldn't handle the magnitude of that.

"You're…you're a very special woman, Janice," he said quietly. "Very rare. Very wonderful. You mean…a great deal to me."

"I care for you, too, Taylor, very much."

"Well, that's…good, that's fine…I guess." Taylor sighed and shook his head. "Hell, Janice, I don't know what to say to you. I'm very confused right now, okay? I *do* know that I don't want to do anything, ever, to hurt you. Do you believe that?"

Janice nodded slowly. "Yes. Yes, I do. I trust you, Taylor, and that's not a statement that I would ever make lightly."

"I realize that, and I thank you."

They fell silent again. Darkness dropped over the splendor of nature's sunset like a heavy curtain, then millions of stars began to twinkle in the black-velvet sky. Taylor merged into the heavy traffic of the city.

The silence in the car continued, but it shifted, changed, began to simmer, then crackle with a sensuality that was nearly palpable as they drove closer and closer to Janice's house.

They became acutely aware of each other, of the small distance separating them, of the tantalizing heat of desire that was beginning to thrum low and insistent in their bodies.

This weekend, Janice thought, this wondrous weekend, wasn't over yet. Not yet. Taylor would carry her suitcase into the house, stand in her living room, prepare to say good-night to end their two days together. He'd probably kiss her, once, maybe twice, then leave.

She'd close up the house, prepare for bed, slip between the cool sheets, then stare up into the darkness.

Alone.

Missing Taylor.

Aching for Taylor.

Wanting to make love with Taylor Sinclair.

That was how it would be.

Unless…

Janice looked out the side window of the car, her heart and mind racing.

Unless she gathered her courage and made it clear to Taylor that she wanted him beyond measure, that she wanted to make love with him through the hours of the night.

Could she do it? Be that bold? Brave? Worldly? Would she regret taking such a momentous step when she faced what she'd done in the light of the new day?

Janice turned her head to look at Taylor again, drinking in the sight of his handsome, rugged profile, of his strong but gentle hands as they held the steering wheel, of his long, powerful legs and broad shoulders.

Along with the heat of desire that was pulsing deep within her, there was now a gentle warmth, a contented and firm sense of rightness about making love with this magnificent and complex man.

What did that mean? she wondered. Was she falling in love with Taylor? Oh, what did it matter how deeply her feelings for him went?

When Taylor walked out of her life, which he would surely do, she would cry the tears of despair, then gather her inner courage and fortitude, and move forward with her life once again.

Alone.

But as the days, weeks, months, then years passed, she would hold fast to the wondrous memories of what she'd shared with Taylor. Those glorious remembrances would be enough, would have to be, somehow, to see her through the remainder of her days.

No, she didn't know if she was falling in love with Taylor Sinclair. She had no experience in recognizing that momentous emotion. But that she cared for him very, very much was a given, a truth so fiercely intense it seemed as though she could actually touch it, hold it in her hands like a fragile treasure to be cherished.

Oh, yes, she wanted to make love with Taylor this night and end the special weekend they'd spent together with the ultimate intimacy between woman and man.

And she would have no regrets at dawn's light.

She had one wish left from the imaginary genie, Janice thought suddenly. Just one.

Oh, little genie, she whispered in her heart and mind. *I just couldn't bear it if Taylor turned me away, rejected me, didn't desire me as much as I do him. Please, genie, have him accept me just as I am, totally, completely, joyously. Let us have this night together, genie. Please.*

As Taylor drove into Janice's driveway, she drew a steadying breath, then willed her heart to quiet its wild tempo.

This was it, she thought. And this was very, very right.

In the living room, Janice snapped on a lamp, then sat on the sofa with the box containing the crystal hummingbird statue she'd purchased in Prescott. She removed the delicate creation and looked over at Taylor where he stood by the front door holding her suitcase.

"Just put that suitcase down anywhere," she said, smiling. "I must find the perfect place for this, and I'd like your opinion. On the mantel here in the living room? What do you think?"

Think? Taylor thought dryly. Janice wanted him to have an intelligent, rational thought somewhere in the jumbled mess called his mind? Not a chance.

"I don't know," he said, lifting one shoulder in a shrug. He set the suitcase on the floor. "Didn't you say that you have a picture of hummingbirds over your bed? Maybe the statue should go in the same room."

Dear heaven, Janice thought as a tantalizing shiver coursed through her. Taylor was suggesting that they go into her bedroom. Oh, yes, this was definitely it, the moment. She had to be worldly, sophisticated. And she would be, if her trembling legs supported her when she attempted to stand.

"Well, let's go see, shall we?" she said, getting to her feet rather tentatively.

As Taylor followed Janice down the hall, he shook his head.

If this scenario was taking place with anyone but Janice, he'd be wondering if she kept coffee in the house for him to brew in the morning. There they were, marching like little soldiers toward her bedroom, her bed.

But this *was* Janice, and their destination didn't mean anything more than selecting a place to put a pretty souvenir from their trip up north.

Janice was so innocent, so naive, didn't have a clue as to what the male population in general would assume from this invitation to enter her bedroom. Man, oh, man, he'd throttle any guy who tried to take advantage of Janice's lack of knowledge of how the game was played.

They entered the bedroom and Janice crossed the dark room to turn on the small lamp on the nightstand, casting a soft, rosy glow over the expanse.

"Very nice." Taylor swept his gaze around the room, unable to keep from lingering an extra moment on the king-size bed.

Janice set the statue in the center of the round table next to the slipper rocker, then straightened and looked at Taylor.

"How's that?" she said.

He walked forward slowly, stopping about two feet in front of her. He looked at the picture of the two hummingbirds hanging over the bed, the statue, then met Janice's gaze.

"Perfect," he said, nodding.

Okay, Sinclair, get the hell out of here. Now.
"Yep, it's dandy."

Good night, Janice. Goodbye, Janice. Sleep well, Janice. Sinclair, move it.

Janice pulled her heavy braid forward and removed the rubber band, dropping it onto the table next to the crystal hummingbirds. She began to draw her fingers through her hair, freeing it from the braid.

"I agree," she said. "That's where the statue belongs." She paused. "Here. In my bedroom. I'll see it every night and every morning. And, Taylor? When I look at it, I'll remember this weekend I spent with you. Every detail. Every precious moment, every memory of it."

Taylor smiled slightly and nodded, realizing that a strange, achy sensation had closed his throat, making it impossible to speak.

Janice was incredible, he thought. She took nothing for granted. He'd spent hundreds of dollars a pop to show a woman a good time over a weekend, only to have said woman thank him breezily, as though it had all been what was expected of him.

But Janice? They'd tromped around a dinky little town in the mountains, for Pete's sake, then sat on a scratchy blanket on the grass on the square and had a picnic.

And there she stood, sincerity ringing in her voice as she expressed her gratitude for his providing her with such splendid memories.

He felt so humble, so awed by the realness, rareness, the innocence and honesty she continually exhibited. There was nothing phony, nor manipulative about her. She was just Janice.

And she was wonderful.

But...but what in the hell was she doing to her hair?

Taylor's heart seemed to skip a beat, then started again in a wild tempo as Janice fanned her fingers at the nape of her neck beneath her hair. She lifted, then floated, the golden cascade forward to spill over her breasts in shimmering waves.

Taylor swallowed heavily. "What are you doing? I mean... Lord, Janice, what are you doing?"

"I want to end this weekend with the most glorious memory of all," she said softly. "I want to make love with you, Taylor."

"But..." Taylor started, then stopped, his mind racing.

No! he thought frantically. He couldn't take this step with Janice. He couldn't! He was already an emotional wreck, battling with himself over the depth of his feelings for her, and his inability to keep from falling in love with her.

And if he *made* love with her, shared that intimate union?

No! He needed to put distance between himself and Janice Jennings, snatch his heart away from her feminine clutches, and somehow, *somehow,* fall *out* of love with her before it destroyed him.

But, oh, how he wanted her.

Janice closed the short distance between them

and circled Taylor's neck with her arms. He kept his hands curled into tight fists at his sides.

"Don't you want me, Taylor?" Janice whispered. "I'm not asking for promises. There are no strings attached. There's just now, this night, which is ours." She brushed her lips over his. "Do you, Taylor? Want me?"

And Taylor's fragile thread of control snapped.

With a groan of need that rumbled from deep in his chest, he buried his hands in Janice's silken hair and brought his mouth down hard onto hers, parting her lips, delving his tongue into the sweet darkness to meet her tongue.

Oh, Taylor, yes, Janice thought dreamily, then gave way to her rising passion.

The kiss was fire, flames licking through them with a heated flash that consumed them instantly. It was desire beyond anything they had ever known before. It was rich, and real and theirs.

Taylor raised his head a fraction of an inch, took a sharp breath, then slanted his mouth in the opposite direction, claiming Janice's lips once more. He drank of her, savored her, filled himself with the very essence of her.

Slowly and so reluctantly he broke the kiss, then cradled Janice's face in his hands, looking directly into her eyes.

"Are you sure about this?" he said, hearing the gritty quality of his voice. "You'll have no regrets? I couldn't handle it, Janice, if you were sorry that we took this step."

"No regrets," she said whisper-soft. "No promises asked, nor given."

"You know I want you," he said.

But he loved her, too, his mind hammered, and he shouldn't be doing this. It was wrong, so damn dangerous, but he didn't have the inner strength to walk away. Not now. Not tonight. It was too late. He'd face the ramifications of his actions tomorrow.

Tonight was his.

And Janice's.

Together.

"And I want you, Taylor," Janice said. "More than I can even begin to tell you."

Taylor nodded, then outlined the perfect shape of her moist lips with the tip of his tongue. Janice shivered from the tantalizing caress. He dropped his hands from her face and gripped bunches of the material of her tunic, inching it upward.

Janice moved her hands from his neck to his forearms.

"No," she said. "I'm going to turn off the light."

"But I want to see you."

"No, Taylor, please. I need you to make love with *me,* the woman I am, the one you know as a person. Your acceptance of me, your want of me, has nothing to do with how I look. I don't expect you to understand but, please, grant me this request. Please, Taylor?"

"Sweetheart…" He stared up at the ceiling for a long moment, then smiled when he met her gaze again. "Right now I'm putty in your hands. I'd rob a bank for you if you asked me to. Turn off the light."

"Thank you," she said, matching his smile.

Janice crossed the room to the bed, threw back the spread and blanket to reveal mint-green sheets, then snapped off the lamp on the nightstand. Darkness fell instantly over the room.

The only sound was the rustle of clothes being removed and the echo of racing hearts in their ears.

Their eyes adjusted to the darkness, making it possible to close the distance between them and reach eagerly for the one they ached for, needed, wanted beyond measure.

A sigh of pure pleasure escaped Janice's lips as she stepped into Taylor's embrace, her breasts crushing with a sweet pain against the hard wall of his chest. His skin was moist and covered with crisp curls that caused her breasts to tingle. His legs were so powerful and his arousal was heavy and full.

He wanted her, Janice's heart and mind sang. Without seeing her, judging her appearance, this magnificent man wanted her. *Her*.

Taylor sought and found Janice's lips as his hands roamed over her dewy, velvet soft skin. The darkness heightened his senses, creating the most erotic, sensual aura he'd ever experienced.

He could feel Janice's breasts pressed to his chest, the womanly bounty far more than he'd ever imagined she was hiding beneath her baggy clothes.

He inhaled her lingering scent of delicate flowers.

The gentle curve of her hips, the slope of her buttocks, were so feminine, making him acutely aware of his masculinity.

He heard a little whimper of need escape Janice's throat and rejoiced in the knowledge of how very much she wanted him. *Him.*

She tasted like sweet nectar as their tongues dueled, stroked, in a rhythm that was so sensuous it threatened to push him over the edge of his control.

Taylor tore his mouth from Janice's and spoke close to her lips, his voice rough with desire.

"Janice…"

"Yes," she whispered, then grasped one of his hands and led him to the bed.

Taylor followed Janice onto the bed, stretching out next to her, one hand splayed on her flat stomach.

Questions began to nudge his passion-laden mind. Why was Janice insisting on the darkness? Why wouldn't she allow him to see her in the glow from the small lamp on the nightstand?

What was she hiding? What was she afraid of? Did this mean that she didn't trust him completely in some way? Why—

Janice skimmed one hand along Taylor's back in a feathery touch, then moved forward to his chest, then lower…lower…

And all rational thought fled Taylor's mind.

He dipped his head to find Janice's mouth, one hand sifting through her glorious hair that he could just barely see fanned out enticingly on the pillow.

Propping his weight on his other forearm, he raised above her, giving him access to her lush breasts. He shifted his mouth to one breast, drawing it in, laving the nipple to a taut bud with his tongue.

"Oh," Janice said with a little puff of breath.

Taylor paid homage to her other breast as his racing heart echoed in his ears. Janice's hands were never still as they touched, fluttered, explored, creating a heated trail over Taylor's body wherever they traveled.

Incredible heat suffused them, burning hotter and hotter, heightening passions to a fever pitch.

There was an otherworldly quality to it all, there in the darkness. It was as though they had been transported to a faraway place where just the slightest glimpse of the other was enough because the feel, the taste, the aroma was all-consuming.

It was strange, foreign, new and…wonderful. It was a body softly feminine and one taut with masculine muscles. It was Janice. It was Taylor. It was glorious.

And the heat burned hotter.

"Taylor, please," Janice said, a near-sob escaping her lips.

"Yes," he said hoarsely.

He moved over her, then entered her, sheathing himself in the moist darkness, filling her, bringing to her all that he was.

"Oh, yes," she whispered.

The ancient dance began in a slow, rocking rhythm, synchronized to perfection. Taylor increased the tempo and Janice matched him beat for beat, lifting her hips to welcome him.

Faster now. Pounding. Thundering in a cadence that caused coils of tension to tighten within them. Hotter. Higher. Reaching…reaching…

They exploded into oblivion seconds apart, holding tightly to each other, calling the name of the one who had been flung far beyond reality with them.

They hovered there for an eternity, savoring, then floated back slowly, slowly to now.

Taylor collapsed against Janice, his energy spent, then he rolled quickly off of her to lie by her side, one arm encircling her waist.

Their hearts quieted. Breathing returned to normal levels. Bodies cooled. They sighed in unison in sated contentment.

Neither spoke. Neither could find the words to describe the wondrous union. Neither wished to break the ethereal spell.

So they slept.

Hours later Taylor stirred as the sound of his name being spoken in a velvety voice reached him in his deep sleep.

"Hmm?" he said foggily.

"It's four in the morning," Janice whispered. "The sun will be up in an hour. You must go, Taylor, while it's still dark. Go now. Please."

"Janice…" he said as he became fully awake.

"Please, Taylor. It will be the perfect ending to

the most glorious night of my life. Please. Leave while it's dark.''

Why? his mind hammered. Ah, Janice, why?

"Yes, all right," he said.

He kissed her deeply, then left the bed. He found his clothes by chance, pulled them on, then leaned over the bed once more.

"Until later, Sleeping Beauty," he said.

"Yes. Thank you, Taylor," she said quietly. "For everything."

He made his way from the room carefully. Minutes ticked by as Janice strained her ears to finally hear the rumble of Taylor's car being started, then driven away.

"Thank you," she said again.

Then she closed her eyes and gave way to blissful slumber.

Chapter Eleven

Janice woke later than usual and hurried through her morning routine. After a shower, she secured the thick bun at the nape of her neck, then dressed in a mustard-colored boxy suit with off-white sturdy shoes.

And through it all, she smiled.

She could not keep the silly grin from forming on her lips, she thought happily. She felt wonderful, so special and cherished, after the glorious love-making with Taylor the previous night.

Taylor had made love with her, just her, the woman, without her beauty entering into what they had shared. What a gift that was, a treasure to keep forever. She had been accepted just for herself, not for what she looked like.

No wonder she was smiling!

In the kitchen, Janice glanced at her watch and frowned, realizing that she'd have to forgo her ritual of drinking her tea while sitting on the patio watching the pair of hummingbirds.

She had time for a half a cup, she decided, pouring the hot tea into a china cup.

She picked it up, blew on the surface to cool it, then wandered over to the door with the hope of catching at least a glimpse of the birds.

"There you are," she said aloud as one hummingbird appeared for breakfast.

She took a sip of tea and waited for the other bird to flutter into sight.

But it didn't come.

Janice's eyes darted in all directions, looking for the second bird.

Where was it? she wondered. Where was its partner, its other half, its soul mate?

A chill coursed through her as she stared at the single bird.

Alone, her mind echoed. There had been two. Now there was only one. Alone.

No, no, she didn't want the delicate little bird to be alone, to go through its day, the remainder of its life without the other one by its side. They belonged together. *Together.*

They had been so perfect, a couple, flying in unison, enjoying their breakfast, then flitting off to meet what adventures the day would bring.

Oh, dear heaven, not alone.

She couldn't bear the thought of a future stretching into infinity, empty, hollow, because Taylor was gone. *They belonged together.* They were partners, the other half of each other, soul mates.

Yes, oh, yes, that was how it should be because she loved Taylor so very much, completely, irrevocably, with an intensity that defied description.

She was in love with Taylor Sinclair.

Janice blinked, then realized her hand holding the cup was shaking so badly the tea was splashing onto the floor. She gripped the cup with both hands and moved to the counter, setting the cup down carefully.

On trembling legs, she made her way to the table, sinking onto one of the chairs. She propped her elbows on the table and dropped her face into her hands.

Dear heaven, she thought frantically, what had she done? How had this happened? When had she lost control over her emotions and fallen in love with Taylor?

She had meant only to have some stolen time with him that would be filled with wondrous memories that she could bring from the treasure chest in her heart and relive when he was gone.

Yes, she would miss him. And, yes, she would cry when he left. But because she hadn't actually loved him, fallen in love with him, the pain of his leaving would soon ease, allowing her to cherish the lovely memories of what they had shared.

But now?

Oh, God, she'd be shattered, devastated, when Taylor walked out of her life.

"Janice, you foolish, foolish woman," she said, raising her head.

She had no one to blame but herself. She had been so positive that she could have an affair with Taylor, weep when he left, then get on with her life as she'd always known it.

She'd honestly believed that the depth of her growing feelings for Taylor didn't matter, because she wouldn't be able to recognize something as foreign as being in love. Therefore, that emotion couldn't touch her should she succumb to it. Oh, such lofty, sophisticated reasonings.

But she wasn't a sophisticated woman after all. She was an emotional child, who didn't have enough experience in life, in living, to keep from having lost her heart to the most magnificent man she'd ever known.

"What am I going to do?" she said, feeling the prickle of threatening tears at the back of her eyes.

No, she wouldn't come apart, dissolve into a weepy mess. She was getting a grip...right now.

Janice got to her feet and began to pace around the kitchen in jerky little steps.

Think. She had to think. Should she end things with Taylor immediately? Tell him she didn't wish to see him again?

She shook her head.

What was the point? She was in love with Taylor, and nothing could erase that fact. The only thing in her favor was that Taylor didn't know that she loved him.

She stopped in front of the door and stared unseeing at the yard beyond, wrapping her hands around her elbows in a protective gesture. She took a deep, steadying breath.

All right. She was calming down, looking at this dismal situation rationally. It was a given that Taylor would end their relationship. He'd return to his world of stunningly beautiful women who operated under the code of behavior in the singles scene.

Yes, she knew that, had known it from the beginning. She was a novelty to Taylor, a woman far different than he was accustomed to, a break in routine. That wasn't cold or tacky on Taylor's part, it was simply how it was. So be it.

But until he actually said goodbye and went back to where he belonged...he was hers. Hers to drink in the sight of, see his smile, hear his laughter, be the recipient of his touch and kiss, share incredibly wondrous lovemaking with.

Hers to love.

Her broken heart would come in time, along with the tears in the long, lonely nights. But she would not be the one to end what they were now sharing. She would savor every precious moment left with Taylor and tuck the memories away gently.

"Yes," she whispered. "That's what I'll do."

She started to turn from the window when something caught her attention. A gasp escaped her lips.

It was the second hummingbird.

It hovered in the air near the first one that was still at the feeder, then side by side they flew away. Together.

"Be happy," Janice said, unable to stop the tears that filled her eyes. "Don't leave each other. Don't be alone, little birds. Stay—" a sob caught in her throat "—together...forever."

The day was a seemingly endless series of nonproductive hours for Taylor. He was edgy, restless, unable to concentrate on the complicated work spread out on his desk at the office.

He'd lost count of how many times he'd reached for the telephone with the intention of calling Janice, only to snatch his hand back at the last second and dismiss the idea.

What would he say to Janice? he thought, dragging both hands down his face. This was not his typical day after. Not even close. Because he'd never in his life *made* love with a woman he was *in* love with.

Taylor leaned his head on the top of the chair and stared at the ceiling.

What in the hell was he going to do? He felt torn, ripped into two jagged pieces.

One part of him was in awe that he, Taylor Sinclair, had actually fallen in love, had found a woman capable of staking a claim on his heart, mind and soul. It was, quite simply, amazing.

But the other half of his psyche?

Fear. Icy, terrifying fear.

To love was to lose, eventually, somehow, that love.

The evidence of that realization was everywhere around him, shouting that truth in a cruel, taunting voice.

He could not, would not, see Janice again. He had to get out of this relationship before it went one step further. Before he—

"Hell," Taylor said, lunging to his feet.

It was too damn late!

He'd already given his heart to Janice Jennings. If he walked out of her life now, *he* would be the cause of losing her, the one to create his own heartache and loneliness.

Should he leave the ending to fate? Stay with Janice for as long as it lasted? Wait for the blow that would cut him off at the knees, smash him to smithereens?

Or should he control the situation, gear up for the pain and tell Janice he was once again nothing more than her accountant?

"Take your pick, Sinclair," he said as he stared out the window. "Hurt like hell now? Or later? Which one suits your fancy?"

Taylor squeezed the bridge of his nose.

Enough of this, he fumed. He was chasing his own muddled thoughts in circles, adding further tangles to the maddening web of confusion.

He'd go visit his father. That would take his mind off his own turmoil. Yes, that was the ticket. He'd pay a call on his dad, give him another pep talk on how great retirement was, focus on someone other than himself. Good plan.

Once again Taylor left the office in a rush with a mumbled explanation for his hasty exit, and once again his secretary shook her head in total bewilderment at her boss's strange behavior.

Clem Sinclair opened the door and stepped back so his son could enter the living room. Clem was holding two hangers in one hand, each hanger displaying a crisp dress shirt.

"Glad you're here," Clem said, closing the door. "You can help me decide."

"Decide what?" Taylor said, yanking the knot of his tie down a couple of inches.

"Which shirt to wear," his father said. "Plain blue? Or white with blue stripes?"

"Depends on where you're going, I guess," Taylor said absently as he slouched onto the sofa.

Clem crossed the room to stand in front of Taylor.

"I'm taking a lovely lady named Mary Alice out for a seafood dinner," Clem said.

Taylor sat bolt upward, his father having his full attention.

"You're what?" Taylor said, his eyes widening.

"You heard me. Which shirt?"

"Forget the damn shirts," Taylor said, getting to his feet. "Are you nuts? Dad, what are thinking? When I said you should concentrate on ideas for filling your idle hours, that didn't include women, for crying out loud."

"Not women, plural. A woman," Clem said calmly. "Mary Alice, to be precise. I met her at the shuffleboard court here in the complex. She's my age, a widow, very pretty, intelligent, has a dandy sense of humor. We're going out for fish and chips."

"No, you are not," Taylor said, slicing one hand through the air.

"Would you stop shouting?" Clem said. "Land's sake, Taylor, what is the matter with you? I thought you'd be tickled about this. You were the one who made it clear I should quit feeling sorry for myself and get on with my life."

"I didn't mean you should hook up with a woman!"

"You're still yelling," Clem said, frowning.

"Damn straight I am," Taylor said. "Dad, please, listen to me. Don't do this to yourself. What if you fall in love with this Mary Whoever?"

"Mary Alice. Her name is Mary Alice Winters." Clem chuckled. "Isn't that fitting? I met her in the winter of my years and her name is Winters. Ah, fate is so fascinating."

"Did you hear what I said?" Taylor went on. "What if you fall in love with her? Do you really want to go through it again when it happens? Haven't you had enough pain and heartache in your life?"

Clem hooked the hangers over the back of a chair, then sat down.

"Put your butt on that sofa, boy," he said, pointing to the piece of furniture. "Right now."

Taylor mumbled an earthy expletive, but did as he was told.

"Now, then," Clem said, lacing his fingers over his chest as he propped his elbows on the arms of the chair. "Let's take this from the top. Quietly." He paused. "Do I want to go through *it* again when it happens? What exactly is this mysterious *it?*"

"Losing," Taylor said, his voice hushed. He took a shuddering breath. "Loving, then losing. That's how it goes, how it happens, every damn time. Through divorce, death, however it comes, it ends."

He shook his head.

"Dad, you know that. *Your wife died.* She was supposed to be with you during your well-earned retirement years. But is she here? Hell, no. She's gone. Long gone."

"My God," Clem said, dropping his hands to his knees and leaning forward. "That's it, isn't it? That's why you've never married. Your I-want an old-fashioned-woman spiel was a bunch of bull to give me something to gnaw on. You're afraid of love, of being in love, aren't you, Taylor? That's the truth of it, isn't it?"

"Yeah, that's the truth of it," Taylor said, his volume rising again. "And with just cause, don't you think? Look around, Dad. Wake up and smell the coffee. How many happily-ever-afters do you see?''

Clem sank back in his chair. ''Oh, Taylor, where did I fail in raising you? How can you possibly believe what you're saying?

''What's the bottom line here? I should never have married your mother, spent those glorious years with her, had you, a wonderful life, because there was a chance it would end sooner than I expected?''

''Yes!'' Taylor shook his head sharply. ''No. Then again... Damn it to hell, every since I fell in love with Janice my brain has been mush, scrambled eggs, totally worthless and... Forget that. What I mean is... Why are you grinning like a fool?''

''You're in love?'' Clem said, beaming. ''With Janice Jennings of Sleeping Beauty? Well, I'll be damned. Isn't that just the finest thing I've ever heard?''

''No!'' Taylor bellowed, getting to his feet. ''I didn't intend to tell you how I feel about Janice and it's beside the point. Haven't you listened to a word I've said?''

''Sit.''

Taylor sat.

''Son, please, you must hear me out,'' Clem said seriously. ''If I had possessed a crystal ball and had seen the future, knew I would lose your mother so early, I would have still married her and pledged my love to her for as long as it was to last.''

''No. No way,'' Taylor said. ''You're not *that*

crazy. You wouldn't have set yourself up for guaranteed heartbreak, Dad.''

"Oh, yes, I would have, Taylor, because the joy, the richness, of what I shared with your mother would weigh far more on the emotional scale. Taylor, there are no guarantees connected with loving someone. You're convinced that losing that love is a given, guaranteed, and you're wrong.''

"But—''

"Taylor, you're sentencing yourself to an empty, lonely life because you're allowing your fears to control your heart and mind. Where's your courage, your inner strength as a man?

"Are you going to walk—no, run—out of Janice Jennings's life because you're so terrified of losing her? Are you going to deprive the two of you of all you could have together?''

"Dad—''

"Oh, son, no, don't do this to yourself. Live, Taylor. Live, and love, and rejoice in every moment you have with the woman who has captured your heart.''

Taylor dragged a restless hand through his hair. "I...I don't know. I need to protect myself against the kind of pain you suffered when Mom died, the heartache I see my friends go through with divorces and—''

"And never know," Clem interrupted, "what it's like to look across the table every morning at a woman who has filled you with the greatest happiness experienced by man. Never hold a baby in your arms, a miracle, that is a result of loving that woman. Never wake from a sound sleep and reach out in the darkness just to touch her, reassure yourself that she's there, bask in the knowledge that you're not alone. Not alone, Taylor."

"But for how long?" Taylor said, his voice choked with emotion. "How long, Dad, before you're alone again? Only this time you're so painfully aware of what is missing, what was there and is now gone. *How long?*"

"It doesn't matter."

"What?"

"When you're in love, Taylor, a heartbeat is a lifetime of happiness. When you're alone and lonely? A tick of time is an eternity. Think about that, Taylor. Look at your Janice, hold her in your arms, and think about that."

The father gazed at the son with love, as the son stared at the father in confusion. Silence fell over the room as they continued to look directly into each other's eyes.

Taylor broke the connection and got to his feet slowly, feeling weary to the bone.

"I've got to go," he said, walking toward the door. He stopped with his hand on the doorknob and turned slightly to look back at his father. "Thanks, Dad. I'll...I'll think about what you said."

Clem nodded.

"And, Dad?" Taylor said, his voice husky. "I vote for the striped shirt. It has more pizzazz."

Clem Sinclair continued to stare at the door after Taylor closed it behind him.

"Be patient with my boy, Janice Jennings," he whispered. "He's worth waiting for, Ms. Sleeping Beauty."

Chapter Twelve

When Taylor left his father's home, he drove, with no particular destination in mind.

A half hour later, he shook his head in self-disgust when he realized he was only two blocks from the Sleeping Beauty boutique.

Two blocks from Janice.

Janice did not keep the shop open late on Monday nights, he knew, time having proven that her customers were still recuperating from the weekend on the first day of the new week and not up to shopping after work.

The clock on the dashboard in the car announced there were forty-five minutes before Janice closed the store and headed home.

Taylor drove to a small park that was located on

the street behind the boutique, wandered around the pretty grounds, then finally settled onto a bench beneath a mulberry tree.

He removed his tie, stuffed it into the pocket of his suit coat, then ran one hand over the back of his neck with a weary sigh.

This was great, he thought dryly. Now he was hiding out behind a tree rather than facing Janice. The woman he loved. The woman who scared the living daylights out of him simply by existing, being who she was.

His Janice.

His Sleeping Beauty.

"Ah, hell." Taylor sighed, a sigh that seemed to come from the very depths of his soul.

When you're in love, Taylor, a heartbeat is a lifetime of happiness. When you're alone and lonely? A tick of time is an eternity. Think about that, Taylor. Think about that… Think about that… Think…

"All right, all right, Dad," Taylor said aloud, frowning deeply.

Alone and lonely. He would, indeed, be exactly that without Janice in his life. He loved her so damn much. He didn't care if she wore awful clothes with clunky shoes, and kept her glorious hair in a tight, unflattering bun. None of that mattered. Not one little bit.

He loved Janice for who she was. She was everything and more that any man could hope to find in his life's partner, his wife, the mother of his children.

There was nothing, *nothing,* about Janice to drive him away. Yes, granted, he was aware that she still had secrets she was keeping from him. There was something haunting her, reasons why she refused to reveal her body in its purest form to him. She didn't trust him totally yet, not yet.

So, okay, that hurt a bit, but he would be patient, give Janice all the time she needed to truly believe in him, and realize he was the real goods.

No, he wasn't at war with himself because Janice was lacking in any way. It was his own fear of losing her that had him confused.

Where's your courage, your strength as a man?

Clem's words echoed in Taylor's mind, once again, causing him to draw a sharp breath, as though he'd been punched in the solar plexus.

Maybe, just maybe, time was the answer for him, too. Maybe he could conquer his fears slowly, with each passing day and night with Janice. Maybe he could—

Taylor was pulled from his tormenting thoughts by a bright red ball rolling on the grass in front of him. Following the ball with gurgling giggles was a little boy, a toddler not completely steady on his feet.

Taylor reached down to pick up the ball and extended it toward the baby.

"Here you go, sport," he said, smiling. "That ball moves faster than you do, doesn't it?"

"Frankie!" a woman said, rushing toward Taylor and the child. She stopped and smiled at Taylor. "I'm sorry if he disturbed you. I turned my back for a second and he was gone."

"Baa," Frankie said, extending his chubby hands toward the ball Taylor held.

"Come on, Frankie," the woman said as Taylor gave the toddler the ball. "Daddy will be home soon, and we want to be there when he arrives."

"You two will be quite a welcoming committee for your husband," Taylor said, looking up at the woman. "He's a lucky man."

"Thank you," she said. "That's a lovely thing to say. Frankie and I are fortunate to have a man like Jim come home to us every night, too." She laughed. "That makes it just about perfect, doesn't it? We're a happy little family, with all of us loving each other."

"Yes," Taylor said. "It's perfect."

The woman scooped up Frankie. "Off we go. Goodbye, and thanks for rescuing Frankie's ball."

"'Bye," Taylor said quietly.

He sat perfectly still, his gaze riveted on the mother and child until they disappeared from view, his mind echoing over and over what the woman had said.

"I give up," he said finally, throwing out his arms. "Frankie, his mom, lucky Jim and a bouncing red ball tipped me over the edge."

Taylor planted his hands on his thighs and pushed himself to his feet.

Janice Jennings, he thought, *I love you. And you're about to be informed of that fact.* Then? Hell, let the chips fall where they may. Time. Maybe that was the key for both him *and* Janice.

With a decisive nod, Taylor strode toward his car.

Janice hummed softly as she moved through the boutique, scrutinizing each rack of merchandise to be certain everything was in order for the next day. Satisfied with what she saw, she started toward the door to lock it, just as Taylor entered Sleeping Beauty.

"Taylor," she said, an instant smile on her face.

"I'm sorry," he said. "I know I should have called you today."

Janice's smile was replaced by a frown. "Why?"

Taylor opened his mouth, closed it, then shook his head as he chuckled.

"Ah, Janice," he said. "You're really something."

And, oh, Taylor, Janice thought, *I love you.* As foolish as it was, it was true. And for as long as Taylor was there, he was hers. They would be together. Just like the hummingbirds.

"The rules are that I should speak with the woman to be assured she's all right the day after the night before," Taylor said, smiling slightly.

"Oh," Janice said. "I didn't know that."

Which was just one of the reasons that he loved her, Taylor thought.

"*Are* you all right?" he said.

Janice smiled. "Yes, thank you." She paused. "Am I supposed to ask you the same thing?"

"No. We guys are on our own, I guess. We're supposedly emotionally tough, or whatever."

"That hardly seems fair."

"No joke," Taylor said dryly.

"Taylor, would you please lock the door before someone comes in? Sleeping Beauty is officially closed for today."

Taylor snapped the lock into place, flipped the sign over to read Closed, then looked at Janice again.

"I need to talk to you," he said, no hint of a smile on his face. "Let's get something to eat. Okay?"

"Talk to me about what? You sound and look awfully serious."

"It's serious business, Janice."

"Oh," she said, a chill sweeping through her. "Well, I'll get my purse. Shall I follow you in my car?"

"No, I'll bring you back here to pick it up."

Janice nodded and went to retrieve her purse and turn off the lights.

What was Taylor going to say to her? she thought, her heart beating with a painful tempo. He looked haggard, tired, like a man with a great burden on his mind and his broad shoulders.

"Listen," Taylor said "I have a new plan. You drive on home and I'll stop and get take-out Chinese food, okay? I'd rather have our conversation in private, not in a crowded restaurant.''

Janice felt the color drain from her face and flicked the lights off quickly, welcoming the shadows that were cast over the store.

"What kind of Chinese food do you like?" Taylor said.

"Anything," she said quietly. "All of it. It doesn't matter.''

"All right. I'll go out the front door, so lock it behind me before you leave through the rear entrance. I'll meet you at your house.''

Taylor walked toward the door, stopped, then came back to where Janice stood by the far wall. He cradled her face in his hands, lowered his head and kissed her so deeply, so intensely, she felt as though her bones were dissolving. He ended the searing kiss and nodded once sharply.

"That's better," he said, his voice gritty. "*Now* I'll leave and go get our dinner. See ya.''

Janice opened her mouth to echo Taylor's farewell, only to realize there was no air left in her lungs. She took a much-needed breath as Taylor went out the front door.

"Taylor Sinclair," she said, stomping across the expanse to relock the door, "you are the most complicated, confusing, unsettling man I have ever met in my entire life.''

She flipped the lock into place, then floated the fingertips of one hand up to rest on her lips, savoring the taste of Taylor, the feel of his mouth on hers, the remembrance of his aroma of fresh air and soap.

"And I love you," she whispered.

After battling the heavy, rush-hour traffic, Janice arrived home, collected her mail, entered the house and went on to her bedroom. She set her purse and the mail on the slipper rocker, then sank onto the edge of the bed.

What should she do? she thought. Stay dressed as she was? Change into a shapeless caftan?

And what about her hair? Leave it in the bun? Twist it into a braid like she'd worn to the picnic in Prescott? Allow it to fall free as she had the night before?

What to do? What to do?

If only she knew what was on Taylor's mind. If he was about to end their relationship, she needed the shield of her boxy suit and severe hairdo. They were a barrier to hide behind, might possibly, somehow, protect her from the full force of the painful words Taylor would be hurling at her.

But what if that *wasn't* what Taylor was going to say? He might have new information regarding the outlet of Sleeping Beauty that was to open in Hamilton House. He might have decided he preferred privacy to discuss financial matters with her.

He'd looked so serious, but accountants were very serious people when it came to money, profit and loss, the whole nine yards.

And that kiss. Heavenly days, that kiss in the

boutique certainly hadn't delivered the message of "Goodbye forever, Janice." That kiss had fanned the embers still smoldering within them from the exquisite lovemaking shared the previous night.

"Oh, Taylor," she said aloud, throwing up her hands. "There are times when I don't understand you one iota."

So, she'd do what felt right to *her,* and simply wait to find out what the serious business was that Taylor wanted to discuss.

It was close to an hour later before Janice heard Taylor's car pull into the driveway. A very long hour that had resulted in her nerves becoming frayed and a stress headache to begin pounding in her temples.

She crossed the living room and flung open the front door before Taylor had a chance to ring the bell.

"Did you go to China for the Chinese food?" she said, surprising herself as she heard the sharp edge to her voice. She sighed in the next instant. "I'm sorry. That was rude. Come in."

Taylor didn't move.

He just stood there, staring at Janice, his racing heart echoing in his ears.

Look at her hair, he thought wildly. He'd seen it falling free last night, but it was still knocking him for a loop as he gazed at it again in all its glory. Gorgeous. Janice's hair was absolutely fantastic. It was sun-kissed wheat, silken and wavy, floating over her breasts and beyond in a sensuous cascade.

Heat was exploding through him. He could feel it beginning to coil hot and low in his body. All because Janice had taken her hair down, freed it from that awful bun.

The rest of her? She was covered from neck to mid-calf in a white, terry-cloth robe that was belted at the waist, giving little clue as to what was beneath the heavy material.

But that hair? He was going up in flames.

"Taylor?"

"Huh? Oh. Right."

He entered the living room and dropped a small, dark blue canvas gym bag on the floor.

"What's that?" Janice said, looking at the bag.

"I stopped at my place and changed into jeans and T-shirt as you can see. I also grabbed my bathing suit and a beach towel," he said. "I thought we might…maybe…go for a swim later. Then again, we might not, depending on how our talk goes. But then again… Ah, hell, forget it. Come on. Let's eat before this stuff gets ice cold."

Taylor strode past Janice and headed for the kitchen. Janice closed and locked the door, stared at the gym bag for a long moment, then followed Taylor's path to the rear of the house.

A short time later, a multitude of little white boxes were spread out on the table. Janice had produced plates and utensils, along with sodas and tall tumblers filled with ice. She and Taylor sat opposite each other, peering into the boxes and inhaling the delicious aromas wafting through the air.

"You must have gotten one of everything on the menu," she said, smiling. "There's enough food here for an army. We should invite your father and my neighbor, Shirley, to join us."

"No," Taylor said sharply.

"I was kidding, Taylor," she said, frowning.

"Sorry," he mumbled.

"Well, now we're even," Janice said. "We've both bitten the other's head off. I do believe that when someone announces they wish to have a very serious discussion, it has a tendency to wreak havoc with the state of people's nerves."

"Yeah. Eat."

They filled their plates, then ate in silence.

He was chewing and swallowing, Taylor thought, but he sure as hell wasn't tasting anything. He was a complete basketcase. He wished he *was* in China, anywhere, except sitting across the table from the only woman he'd ever loved and preparing himself to declare that love. Out loud.

Oh, man, he couldn't do this. It was too big, too powerful and overwhelming. Too damn terrifying.

Where's your courage, your strength as a man?

It flew the coop, Dad, Taylor mentally answered, as his father's words echoed in his mind. *Speak, Sinclair. Say something, anything, to break this oppressive silence.*

"My father has a date tonight," he said. Cripe, that was so lame. He'd made it sound as though

Clem Sinclair taking a lady out for seafood was the news flash of the year. "Yep. Her name is Mary Alice."

"Well, that's nice," Janice said, smiling. "I hope they have a lovely evening."

"So do I...now," he said quietly. "I jumped my dad's case when he first told me he was going out with a woman."

"Why?"

Taylor pushed his plate away, leaned back in the chair and crossed his arms over his chest. He stared up at the ceiling for a long moment, then met Janice's gaze.

"Why?" he repeated. "Because as soon as he told me his plans, my mind went into fast forward, seeing my father falling in love with this Mary Alice woman. Seeing him loving again, then...then losing again, suffering that agony, that soul-deep pain."

"But—"

"That, Janice," he went on, as though she hadn't spoken, "is how I view love, being in love. Has been for as long as I can remember. And this, in case you're missing it, is the serious discussion I wanted to have with you."

"Oh," Janice said, staring at him with wide eyes.

"To love," he continued, his voice slightly raspy, "is to lose. To have it end. Either by death, or divorce, it's over. You're sliced and diced, and bleeding to death emotionally. Therefore, I vowed never to fall in love."

"I see," Janice whispered, an achy sensation gripping her throat.

"But I did." Taylor shifted forward and planted his hands flat on the table. "Fall in love. With you. I...I love you, Janice Jennings."

Time stopped.

Janice felt as though an invisible hand had pressed a button and everything was suddenly frozen in place. Taylor was looking at her with an intense expression on his face, not blinking, not seeming to be breathing.

She was floating outside of herself, she thought hazily. She was watching the scene at the table from afar, marveling at the wonder of it, hearing the echo of Taylor's words over and over in her mind, her heart, her very soul.

I love you, Janice Jennings.

Dear heaven, Taylor loved her, *her,* just as she was. He had not only accepted her without all the outer trappings of beauty, but he had actually, unbelievably, fallen in love with her. For the first time in her life, she was loved for herself, who she was as a person.

And she loved Taylor Sinclair with every fiber of her being.

It was too much, it really was. She had waited an eternity for this gift, had felt it would never come, wasn't hers to have. But it was here. Love. Acceptance. A future of togetherness, just as the hummingbirds had.

It was overwhelming in its magnitude and glory,

more than she had room to embrace within herself. The emotions were flowing rapidly within her, needed an outlet, somewhere to go.

And so, Janice covered her face with her hands and burst into tears.

"Oh, good Lord," Taylor said, jumping to his feet. "Don't cry. Why are you crying? Janice?"

He rushed around the table and dropped to one knee next to Janice's chair. He gripped her gently by the shoulders and turned her toward him.

"Janice? Hey, talk to me. I'm sorry." He shook his head. "What am I sorry about? Man, this is confusing." He eased her hands from her face, then trailed his thumbs over the tears on her cheeks. "Please don't cry. Why are you crying?"

"Because...because you love me," she said, then sniffled. "Me."

"Right." Taylor frowned. "Does this make sense?" He got to his feet, pulling Janice up and into his embrace. "Yes, I love you. I want to be totally honest with you and say that I'm scared down to my socks because I've fallen in love with you but...Janice, there's something missing from this picture."

"There is?" she said, tears still brimming her eyes.

"Definitely." Taylor paused. "What are your feelings for *me?*"

"Oh, Taylor," she said, fresh tears spilling onto her cheeks. "I love you so much."

"No joke? You do?" he said, a smile breaking

across his face. "Well, that certainly helps this crazy situation, doesn't it?" He sobered in the next instant. "It isn't perfect, Janice. We need time to smooth out the wrinkles. The fears I have rush over me and I get shaky, really terrified. And you? Well, you don't trust me, believe in me completely...not yet."

"Taylor, I—"

"Hey, it's okay. We'll take it slow and easy, get accustomed to all this as it comes, one day at a time." He brushed his lips over hers. "One night at a time."

Taylor captured Janice's mouth in a heated kiss. Janice wrapped her arms around his neck and answered the demands of the kiss in total abandon.

The desire within her was matched with such happiness she felt as though she would burst.

I love you, Taylor, her mind hummed.

Ah, Janice, Taylor thought as heated passion rocketed throughout him, *I love you.*

He broke the kiss slowly, so reluctantly, then took a step backward, putting distance between Janice and his aroused body.

"Our dinner is getting cold," he said, smiling.

Janice laughed, her misty eyes sparkling with joy. "Heaven forbid."

They settled onto their chairs again, then their gazes met across the table.

"I'll never forget this moment, Taylor," Janice whispered.

"No, I won't, either," he said quietly.

"I don't think I want any more to eat right now."

"I've had enough, too," he said. "We can stick all these nifty little boxes in the refrigerator and heat it up later."

"Yes."

This was it, Janice thought, feeling her heart increase its tempo. The time had come. Taylor loved her and she must learn to trust him completely with who she really was.

Janice rose and moved to the side of the table. "Would you like to go for a swim, Taylor?"

He nodded and got to his feet. "Sounds good."

With hands that were visibly shaking, Janice pulled the looped belt free on the robe and slipped the heavy material from her shoulders, allowing it to fall into a puddle at her feet.

She stood perfectly still, hardly breathing, wearing a tiny, teal blue, bikini bathing suit.

"Oh...Janice." Taylor's voice was a hoarse whisper and the echo of his racing heart thundered in his ears. "You are so—"

"No," she said, raising one hand palm out. "Don't say it. Please, Taylor, don't say that I'm beautiful. It's just outside packaging. You're in love with me, Janice Jennings, the woman. Isn't that right, Taylor?" A sob caught in her throat. "Isn't it?"

Taylor closed the distance between them in two long strides, gathered Janice into his arms and held her tightly.

"Yes," he said, burying his face in her fragrant

hair. "Yes, don't ever doubt that." He eased her back and framed her face in his hands so he could gaze directly into her tear-filled eyes. "I know you've been hurt very badly in the past and it centers, somehow, on how beau—how you look. It's up to you if you want to tell me about it. If you do, I'll listen. If you choose not to, that's fine."

"Thank you," she whispered.

"No, *I'm* thanking *you*," he said, "for trusting me enough to wear that swimsuit." He smiled. "You don't mind if I appreciate the view a bit, do you?"

"That would be all right, I guess," she said, managing a small smile. "I just might gawk a tad at you in a bathing suit, too."

"Sounds like a plan." Taylor dropped a quick kiss on her lips. "I'll go change my clothes and meet you in the pool."

Janice nodded, said she'd put the food in the refrigerator, and they parted. Taylor retrieved the gym bag from the living room and went into Janice's bedroom. He set the bag on the bed, then dragged both hands down his face.

Unbelievable, he thought. Janice was the most incredibly beautiful woman he'd ever seen. She was perfect, as though she'd been sculpted from the finest ivory marble, then smoothed by the hands of a master artist.

How strange it all was to realize he'd fallen in love with Janice before he knew the extent of her beauty. She was right. It was just outside packaging that encased a warm, loving, intelligent woman.

He was guilty, he knew, of a lifetime of judging the... the wrappings, before approaching a woman. And women did that to him, too, he supposed. They checked him out, deciding if his looks and build passed muster before the come-on-over smile appeared on their faces.

But not this time. Not with Janice.

They'd even made love in the darkness of night, unable to see each other clearly. Exquisite love, more physically intense and emotionally moving than anything he'd ever experienced before.

"Unreal," Taylor said, pulling his T-shirt over his head. "And fantastic."

Lord, how he loved that woman. Janice was so rare, so special. And so very fragile and vulnerable.

He frowned as he continued to shed his clothes.

Who had hurt her? It centered on her beauty, that much was certain, and there was something off base about Janice's mother and—Hell, he didn't know what the story was.

Would Janice ever trust him enough to bare her soul to him? He'd told her it didn't matter if she chose to keep her secrets, but...well, it did matter, it really did. Would she come to love him enough to trust him that much?

Did Janice love him enough to stay by his side forever?

A chill swept through Taylor as he stepped into his white bathing trunks.

Forever? In connection with love? Who was he kidding? He knew the score. The evidence was all around him, everywhere he turned. To love was to lose. Eventually. Somehow. It ended. Was gone. And the heartache lasted an eternity.

"Shut up, Sinclair," he said aloud.

He wasn't dwelling on his fears, not tonight. He had declared his love to a woman for the first time in his life and she'd responded in kind.

This was their night, and nothing was going to mar it. This was a night of memories to make, to keep…forever.

The last traces of a vibrant sunset had disappeared beneath the horizon to be replaced by a velvety black sky sparkling with millions of stars. The automatic timer had switched on the lights in the pool, creating an aqua oasis in the backyard.

When Taylor reached the edge of the pool, Janice was swimming underwater, her hair floating outward like a glorious fan. He stared at her, feeling the jolt of heated desire low in his body as he gazed at the vision of loveliness before him.

Janice surfaced and treaded water, the smile she gave Taylor genuine.

"Are you coming in?" she said. "It's heavenly."

Oh, my gracious, she thought, Taylor in a bathing suit was a sight to behold. He was perfectly proportioned…wide shoulders, nicely muscled arms, narrow hips and long, powerful legs. The hair on his chest was causing her fingertips to tingle with the urge to tangle in the masculine curls. My, my, my.

"I confess, I'm gawking," she said. "You're magnificent, Taylor."

And you are beauty personified, he thought.

"You're not too shabby yourself, ma'am," he said, smiling.

Taylor dove into the water, causing Janice to shriek as a spray of water fell over her. He surfaced in front of her, treading water as she was.

"Catch me if you can," she said, then sank beneath the surface and swam away.

"You're on, mermaid," Taylor said. "Here I come."

They frolicked like carefree children, their joyous laughter carried on a gentle breeze. Half an hour later, Janice gripped the edge of the pool in the deep end with one hand and brushed her hair from her face.

"That's it, that's all," she said. "I'm all tuckered out, mister."

Taylor swam to where she was, bracing his hands on the rolled edging of the pool on either side of her, trapping her between his arms.

"Thank goodness," he said, smiling. "I thought I was going to have to blow my machismo to hell by begging to stop. You're an excellent swimmer."

"It's fun. I enjoy it. It's very relaxing."

"Fun," Taylor repeated, then outlined her lips

with the tip of his tongue. "Enjoyable." He nipped at her lower lip in sensuous little bites. "Relaxing."

"I..." Janice started, then stopped speaking as a frisson of heat feathered down her back.

Taylor claimed her mouth in a searing kiss. She released her hold on the side of the pool and encircled his neck with her hands, his hips with her legs. He tightened his grip on the edging to support their weight and deepened the kiss.

They were on fire, the cool water having no diminishing effect on the heated desire consuming them. They broke the kiss, took sharp breaths, then sought each other's mouths once again, eagerly, hungrily.

Janice's breasts were crushed to Taylor's chest as his arousal pressed heavily against her. Tongues met, darted, stroked, dueled and danced, heightening passions even more.

Taylor reached behind Janice with one hand, undid the bow at the nape of her neck, then unsnapped the thin band of material across her back. He flung the bikini top onto the decking.

Janice's breasts were half above, half below, the surface of the water. Taylor licked the beads of water from the feminine bounty. Janice murmured in pleasure at the tantalizing sensations.

She inched her fingers into his thick, wet hair, urging him nearer, offering more. He lifted one breast to draw the nipple into his mouth, laving it with his tongue.

"Oh, Taylor," Janice whispered as the building heat within her flared hotter.

Taylor raised his head to look into her eyes. "I want you, Janice."

"Yes. I want you, too, Taylor."

With an economy of motion they slithered out of their suits, then Janice wrapped her legs around Taylor's hips again. He slid one hand down her glistening back to position her, then entered her, thrusting deeply within her.

She flung her head back and closed her eyes, savoring…savoring…savoring…

It was ecstasy.

Taylor increased the tempo, surging into her, one hand on the edge of the pool to keep them afloat, the other at the small of Janice's back.

The pounding rhythm caused heated spirals to tighten within them, hotter, then hotter yet. Janice clung to Taylor's shoulders as she matched the wild tempo.

Until…

"Taylor!"

"Ah, Janice!"

They were flung upward to greet the welcoming stars in the sky, then spun through the glittering heavens, holding fast to the one making the wondrous journey with them.

Back they came…down…down…

Taylor lost his grip on the edge of the pool and their lips met beneath the surface of the water. He wrapped one arm around Janice's waist and broke the top of the water again, grabbing the edge of the pool. She nestled her head on his shoulder.

"Oh, Taylor," she whispered.

"I know." He took a much-needed breath, then chuckled. "Maybe in our next life we'll be dolphins."

"No," she said softly. "I'd like us to be hummingbirds."

Chapter Thirteen

The following weeks flew by.

Janice and Taylor were together every evening...and night. Sometimes they went out to dinner; other evenings they brought food into either Janice's house, or Taylor's apartment. On several occasions they attempted to cook together, soon realizing that neither was particularly proficient in the chore.

Janice discovered to her amused delight that Taylor was a pack rat. While basically tidy, he had a multitude of neat stacks of newspapers and magazines in the room in his apartment he'd designated as his den.

"You never know when you might need to review an article you've read in the past," he'd explained. "You just never know."

"I see. But how would you remember where you read it?"

"Oh. I never thought of that. Well, I guess I'd just dive in and search for it."

"Ah."

They shopped for groceries, spent lazy hours by Janice's pool, and went out to dinner one night with Clem and Mary Alice.

"I just double-dated with my father," Taylor said, when he and Janice had returned to her house. "Is that weird?"

"I think it's sweet. Your father and Mary Alice seem very happy together."

Taylor had pulled Janice into his embrace and looked directly into her eyes.

"Like father like son," he said. "I'm a very happy man, Janice Jennings."

"And I'm a happy woman, Taylor Sinclair. I never dreamed I could feel this way."

They made love each night, reaching for the other eagerly, as though it had been days instead of hours since they'd shared the glorious intimacy.

In the morning, Taylor would lie in bed and watch Janice dress, seeing the sensuous lingerie from Sleeping Beauty covered by the familiar boxy suit. See her glorious hair twisted into the severe bun at the nape of her neck.

Whenever they had ventured out, including the evening spent with Clem and Mary Alice, Janice had worn her frumpy uniform. It wasn't until she was alone with Taylor that she freed her hair and wore a teeny bikini, or shorts and a form-fitting top.

Taylor never questioned the ritual, nor urged Janice to dress differently when they were in public. She was Janice, and that was all that mattered.

When the deep-seated fears about being in love assaulted Taylor during the day, he picked up the telephone and called Janice, the mere sound of her voice chasing away the inner chill consuming him.

Just as his father had said, Taylor woke often in the night to reach over and touch Janice where she slept peacefully beside him, rejoicing in the fact that she was there, she was his.

He'd totally conquer his fears in time, he silently vowed. And in time, Janice would learn to trust him completely, share her innermost secrets with him.

The construction of the specialty shops in Hamilton House was progressing rapidly. Andrea and Brandon drove down the mountain so Andrea could meet with Janice to map out an advertising campaign for the Sleeping Beauty outlet in Prescott. They worked together at the boutique between customers while Taylor and Brandon played golf.

One evening they all met for dinner at a small Italian restaurant.

It was three weeks to the day since Janice and Taylor had declared their love for each other. Taylor lifted his glass of wine in a silent toast to Janice. She knew, she just somehow knew, what he was acknowledging, and clinked her glass to his, smiling at him warmly.

As the foursome waited for dessert to be served, Janice and Andrea headed for the ladies' room.

"Okay," Brandon said, looking at Taylor. "I held myself back during all those hours on the golf course, didn't say a word, didn't ask any questions. But now that I've seen you and Janice together during dinner—hell, Sinclair, you're in love with that woman and she loves you."

Taylor nodded. "Yep."

"That's it?" Brandon said, his eyes widening. "Just 'yep?' You're not going to deny it, argue the point, tell me I'm out of my mind?"

"Nope."

"I'll be damned," Brandon said, grinning. He sobered in the next instant. "So when are you going to do it? Wake up Sleeping Beauty, mighty prince?"

"What do you mean?" Taylor said, frowning.

Brandon folded his arms on the top of the table and leaned toward Taylor.

"Come on, buddy," Brandon said. "Janice has all the makings of a beautiful woman, but she's still hiding behind those ridiculous clothes. You're in love, for crying out loud. Isn't it time for her to be true to herself? Be who she really is?"

"She steps from behind those protective walls when we're alone, Brandon," Taylor said quietly. "She's even more beautiful than I could have ever imagined. She's absolutely sensational."

Brandon narrowed his eyes. "Why aren't you encouraging her, helping to give her the confidence, to show her true self in public?''

Taylor lifted one shoulder in a shrug. ''That choice is up to Janice. We never discuss it.''

''Taylor, I can't believe you're actually doing this,'' Brandon said, shaking his head.

''Doing what?'' Taylor said, obviously confused.

''Man, oh, man, who are you kidding? Have you honestly convinced yourself that you're not touching the subject of Janice's appearance in public out of love and respect for her wishes?''

''Well, yeah, that's exactly it.''

''Bull,'' Brandon said, smacking the table with the palm of one hand. ''You like the status quo because it's safe. No man is going to look twice at Janice now, the way she presents herself. As far as the male populace goes, she's an invisible woman.

''Hell, no, you're not going to wake up Sleeping Beauty, encourage her to be the woman she really is for public scrutiny. Why run the risk of having another man catch her attention while he's appreciating the view?''

''Now wait just a damn minute, Hamilton,'' Taylor said none too quietly. He quickly glanced around the restaurant and lowered his voice when he spoke again. ''I don't like what you're implying here.''

''If the shoe fits, Sinclair. I think you're afraid of losing Janice, so you're taking the ugly duckling out in public and keeping the beautiful swam all for yourself. Janice deserves better than that from you.''

Before Taylor could say more, Andrea and Janice approached the table and settled back onto their chairs. The waiter appeared with the sherbet they'd requested for dessert.

Andrea glanced at Brandon, Taylor, then back to Brandon.

"What's going on?" she said. "You two look like grumpy bears."

"What?" Brandon said. "Oh, it's nothing, sweetheart. We got into a heavy discussion about baseball teams, that's all."

"Heavy," Janice said merrily. "Are you two going to duke it out in the parking lot?"

"Don't tempt me," Taylor said, still glowering at Brandon.

"Some people need to come out of the ether," Brandon said, matching Taylor's expression.

"And some people need to mind their own business," Taylor retorted.

"Fine," Brandon said, raising both hands. "You just let what is sleeping stay asleep. You have to live with your conscience, not me."

"You've got that straight, Hamilton," Taylor said.

"Would you stop it?" Andrea said. "You sound like squabbling little boys. Besides that, you're not making any sense. What baseball team is sleeping...or whatever?"

"Never mind," Brandon said, sighing. "I give up."

"Good," Andrea said. "Eat your sherbet."

"Men certainly take baseball seriously," Janice said.

"Mmm," Taylor said, then stuck his spoon into the dessert.

Hours later Taylor lay next to Janice in her bed, staring up at the ceiling. Janice murmured in her sleep and he reached over to stroke her hair gently until she stilled again. He glanced at the clock on the nightstand, then frowned as he slid his hands beneath his head.

It was after two-thirty in the morning, and he hadn't slept a wink, nor did he expect to sleep the sleep of the innocent at all that night.

Because he was guilty as sin.

He'd replayed in his mind over and over the heated conversation he'd had with Brandon in the restaurant. His anger had flared anew at Brandon's off-the-wall accusations.

But as the dark, solitary hours had passed, he'd examined his motives with stark honesty and faced the truth. Everything Brandon had accused him of was true.

He sighed, pulled his hands free and dragged them down his face, before dropping his arms heavily onto the bed.

He did *not*, he now knew, want Janice to display her beauty for anyone but him.

If she stayed hidden beneath her frumpy clothes while in public, no man would give her a second look. The world and all it could offer her would remain unknown to her. She would stay by *his* side, where she now was, where she belonged.

The risk of losing Janice was greatly diminished if her outward appearance continued as it was. It was so much safer this way, helped keep the chill of fear at bay.

He hadn't said, or done, one thing to encourage Janice to step from behind her walls and embrace her feminine attributes beyond when she was alone with him.

He was rotten to the core.

But, damn it, he loved Janice so much, couldn't bear the thought of losing her. Why couldn't they just continue on the way they were? Janice was obviously happy and heaven knew he was.

Sure. They'd just keep on, keeping on, and Brandon Hamilton could take a flying leap.

Wrong, Taylor thought in the next instant. That wasn't love as it was meant to be. That was control, manipulation.

Now that he'd faced the truth, there was nowhere to hide from it.

He had to love Janice enough to run the risk of losing her.

He had to allow her, encourage her, to blossom like a delicate, exquisite flower opening its petals to the beckoning sun. It would take every bit of inner strength and courage that he possessed as a man, but he had to do it. He had to.

"Ah, hell, " Taylor said, then closed his eyes.

Sleep finally claimed him, but it was plagued with tormenting dreams of searching for Janice in a thick fog. Looking for her frantically, but not finding her.

Because she wasn't there.

She was gone.

At breakfast the next morning in Janice's kitchen, Taylor sipped from a mug of steaming coffee while sitting opposite Janice at the table.

"You don't want anything to eat?" she said.

"No, just coffee," he said. "I'm not hungry."

"That's unusual for you, Taylor."

"Yeah, well." He lifted one shoulder in a shrug. "Listen, the first day I came into the boutique I saw a brochure on your counter for an art exhibit at a classy gallery."

"Oh, yes, I remember that," Janice said, then took a swallow of tea. "I thought I might find something for one of my walls. You have wonderful pieces of art in your apartment."

"Collecting fine art is one of my hobbies. I received that same invitation in the mail. The showing is Saturday night. Would you like to go?"

"I'd love to," she said, smiling.

"It starts at eight o'clock. We could have a late supper after we've been to the gallery."

"Perfect." Janice glanced at her watch. "I must

dash. I have a couple of boxes to unpack before I open the store.'' She got to her feet. ''Enjoy your coffee and say hello to the hummingbirds for me if you see them.''

Taylor rose to stand in front of her and framed her face in his hands.

''Janice, you know that I love you, don't you?'' he said, looking directly into her eyes.

''Yes, I believe you love me, Taylor.'' She paused and frowned. ''Is something wrong? You're not hungry and now you seem so tense, so serious.''

''I... Well, I'm behind on my work at the office because I took the day off to play golf with Brandon. I think I'd better stay late there tonight and attempt to catch up. I'll call you, but I won't see you this evening.''

''Oh.'' Janice laughed. ''I'm tempted to pout. You've spoiled me during these weeks and I'll miss you terribly, Taylor.''

''That's because I'm such a terrific guy, an exemplary human being,'' he said, a slight edge to his voice.

''Taylor? What is it? You just don't seem like yourself this morning.''

He brushed his lips over hers, then dropped his hands to smooth the lapels of her oversize suit jacket.

''There's just something I need to...correct. And I will.'' He nodded. ''Yes, I'm overdue to set things to rights.''

''I'm totally confused.''

"Go to work, my Sleeping Beauty," he said, managing to produce a passable smile. "I'll call you later."

After they'd shared a long, desire-evoking kiss, Janice left the house. Taylor wandered over to look out the rear doors of the kitchen, but the humming-birds were nowhere to be seen.

"It's time to wake up, Sleeping Beauty," he said quietly, feeling as though the weight of his words was crushing him. "The problem is, there are a helluva lot of princes in this world. Oh, God, Janice, don't pick one of them instead of me. Please."

By Saturday morning, Janice was restless and edgy, her nerves frayed.

She had not seen Taylor since breakfast on Thursday morning. He'd telephoned several times, but the conversations had been brief. During one call yesterday, he'd announced that an out-of-town client was coming into Phoenix, and Taylor needed to take the man to dinner that night to discuss business.

He would pick Janice up just before eight o'clock the following evening, he said, and they would go to the gallery showing.

Janice roamed aimlessly around the house, unable to concentrate, or sit still.

Something was wrong with Taylor, she thought for the umpteenth time. He was acting so strangely, so distant. There was a strain, a weariness in his voice when they spoke on the telephone, heightening her sense of gloom. Something just wasn't *right* between them.

"Oh, Taylor," Janice said, pressing trembling fingertips to her temples. "What is it? What's wrong, my love?"

In the beginning of their relationship she'd been resigned to the fact that she was on borrowed time with Taylor, that he would soon tire of her and leave, go back to the world where he had always belonged.

But increasingly she no longer felt that way, wasn't waiting for the inevitable goodbye. No, oh, no, not since Taylor had declared his love for her. Not since the glorious days and nights they'd spent together.

She'd begun to dream, hope, pray, of a future, a forever, with Taylor Sinclair.

But now? Oh, saints above, what on earth was wrong with Taylor?

Janice sank onto the sofa in the living room and sighed deeply.

Her lack of sophistication was rearing its unsophisticated head. She was acting like a child, a Nervous Nelly, unable to cope with the slightest change in routine in her relationship with the man she loved.

Taylor was a human being, for mercy's sake, with a demanding career, a life beyond just focusing his undivided attention on her. He was busy at the moment, that's all, was tending to work.

She had to move past her insecurities and doubts.

That she was lacking in experience in man and woman matters wasn't Taylor's fault, and he mustn't be made to pay the price for it.

"Have you got that, Janice?" she said aloud. "Get your act together. Right now."

She would see Taylor tonight and they would have a fabulous time. Everything was fine, just fine.

The sound of a vehicle turning into the driveway pulled Janice from her thoughts. She got to her feet and went to the window to see a van from a private delivery service come to a halt.

A man in a uniform soon crossed the yard, carrying a large, flat silver-colored box adorned with an enormous silver bow.

"Goodness," she said, heading toward the door. "Whatever can *this* be?"

After signing for the delivery, Janice closed the door and carried the box to the sofa. She slipped a small white envelope from beneath the bow and took out a silver-edged card.

"'I'll see you tonight,'" she read aloud. "'Looking forward to it. Love, Taylor.'"

A soft smile formed on her lips. Taylor had missed her these past couple of days as much as she had missed him. He was even sending her a special gift to let her know that he was anticipating being with her once again.

This was so special, so caring. She'd gotten herself all in a dither over nothing.

"Oh, Taylor," she said, gazing at the card, "I

love you so very much.'' She paused. ''Well, let's see what my surprise is.''

She set the card on the coffee table and began to lift the lid off the glittering box.

Taylor drove just above the speed limit, tapping his fingers on the steering wheel along with a peppy tune playing on the radio.

He was so eager to see Janice that he felt like a kid who was about to pick up his prom date. Well, hell, he didn't care how ridiculous he was acting, he was on top of the world.

He nodded decisively.

He'd done it. He'd gathered his courage, shoved aside his own chilling fears and done it. Once he'd stopped shaking in his shorts, he'd begun to feel good, calm, having a greater sense of understanding of the depths and intensity of *his* love for Janice.

His Sleeping Beauty.

Sure, what he'd set in motion was risky, but anything of the magnitude of what he and Janice shared was worth laying it all on the line for. He had to believe in her, in himself, and what they had together.

He was crumbling into dust his philosophy that to love was to lose, and sending it scattering into the wind, never to haunt him again.

He and Janice would have it all. Nothing, *nothing*, could tear them apart.

Taylor turned into Janice's driveway, shut off the ignition and got out of the car. He strode quickly across the stepping stones as he counted down the seconds until he would take Janice, the woman he loved with every breath in his body, into his arms and kiss her.

He pressed the doorbell and waited for his beloved to appear.

Chapter Fourteen

Even though Janice had heard the familiar rumble
of Taylor's car as it arrived at the house, she still
jerked when the doorbell chimed. On trembling legs
that threatened to give way beneath her, she crossed
the room.

In the first second after she opened the door, she
registered the fact that Taylor looked magnificent
in a dark suit, crisp white shirt and dark tie. In the
next instant she watched the broad smile on his face
change into a deep frown.

"Janice?" he said. "What—"

"Come in," she said quietly, stepping back to
allow him to enter.

After she closed the door, they faced each other,
Taylor's gaze sweeping over her in a quick, but
thorough perusal.

She knew what he was seeing, Janice thought dismally. She was wearing a black, baggy suit, gray blouse and black oxfords. Her hair was in a severe bun. Her eyes were red-rimmed and puffy from having cried long and hard.

"I don't understand," Taylor said, still frowning. "You look like you've been crying. Are you ill, not feeling well? No, that doesn't make sense. If you were sick, you'd be in a robe or something, but you're dressed to go out except... Didn't you receive the surprise I sent you?"

Janice lifted her chin and wrapped her hands around her elbows.

"Oh, yes, Taylor," she said, "I certainly did receive your *surprise.*"

She moved around him and hurried to sink onto one of the chairs. Taylor followed, then hesitated when he saw the open silver box on the coffee table. He sat on the sofa.

"Talk to me," he said. "Didn't you like the dress? I spent a great deal of time picking it out, because I wanted it to be perfect for you."

"It's a lovely dress," she said, wishing her voice didn't hold the echo of tears. "It's the exact shade of blue as my eyes. It would cling to my curves, give a teasing glimpse of the tops of my breasts and... It's subtly sexy.

"Oh, and let's not forget the other part of the *surprise,* Taylor. The certificate for a complete makeover. My hair was to be cut and styled to best accentuate my face, my makeup applied to perfection. I was even to receive a cute little cosmetic bag to carry my makeup in. My goodness, you thought of everything.''

"But?" Taylor said, turning his hands palm up. "You're obviously upset. What did I do wrong here?"

"Oh, nothing," Janice said, her voice ringing with sarcasm. "Nothing at all. You just lied to me, betrayed me, ended up being like everyone else who I've ever trusted and believed in."

"What?" he said, obviously confused.

"Was it Brandon who pushed you over the edge of your tolerance? Was that what you two were glaring at each other about at the restaurant? Did he give you a bad time about being with a drab and unattractive woman? Was that the last straw, Taylor?"

"Janice, for God's sake, I didn't send you these things for *me*." He swept one hand in the direction of the glittering box. "I did it for *you*."

"Please, you're insulting my intelligence."

"It's true, damn it! Yes, Brandon jabbed at me, but not the way you're thinking. I was forced to admit that I liked the idea that I was the only one to see how incredibly beautiful you really are."

"I hate being beautiful," Janice said, nearly shrieking. "Haven't you figured that out by now?"

"Only in bits and pieces, because you haven't shared your secrets with me. I know you've been hurt in the past somehow because of your beauty, but—"

"And now I've been hurt in the present because of it," she interrupted. "You wanted a beautiful woman on your arm at that gallery tonight, didn't you, Taylor? Didn't you?"

"This isn't about me," he said, his volume rising. "You deserve to enjoy your femininity to the fullest. I was attempting to encourage you, be supportive of that. Lord, Janice, I never meant to hurt you. I just wanted you to be…"

"Beautiful," she yelled, getting to her feet.

"Calm down. Please? I'm totally lost here. I just don't understand what I've done to cause you such pain, to upset you like this."

Janice sank back onto the chair and took a steadying breath. When she spoke again, her voice was flat and low, void of emotion.

"Then allow me to enlighten you, Mr. Sinclair. I'll tell you a bedtime story. Yes, this is the story of Janice Jennings, who was never a child, not really. From the time she was three years old she was dragged from one beauty pageant to another, put on display, judged by strangers, who would determine if she was beautiful enough to be accepted, to win the prize."

Taylor stared at Janice, hardly breathing, his heart thundering.

"My mother," she went on, "saw me as an object, a means to an end. My beauty, she informed me continually, was all that mattered, was all that was important. My beauty would get me what I deserved to have. She never hugged or kissed me, never said that she loved me. She just told me how beautiful I was.

"I had no friends, wasn't allowed to play with other children for fear that I might skin my knee or get a bruise. I never...I never even got to play hopscotch. I'd press my nose to the window and watch the kids on the sidewalk. Oh, how I wanted to play hopscotch."

Taylor's heart ached for the child he could see so vividly in his mind's eye. The lonely, unloved, manipulated child. He could feel the flash of fury consuming him, directed toward the mother who had exploited her daughter, hurt her so damn much.

"I never dated," Janice went on, bringing Taylor from his raging thoughts, "didn't go to the mall with giggling girlfriends, didn't talk on the telephone about boys in adolescent whisperings. I just went to school, came home and prepared for the next beauty pageant. Maybe, *maybe,* I thought, if I was judged beautiful enough, my mother would love me."

This wasn't a bedtime story, Taylor thought as a strange tightness gripped his throat. It was a horror story. He wanted to go to Janice, hold her, comfort her, make everything all right.

"When I was eighteen," Janice said, "my mother introduced me to a very wealthy man in his middle forties. Walter was captivated by my beauty and innocence. Within weeks after meeting him, he asked me to marry him. My mother accepted his proposal on my behalf."

"What?" Taylor said, his voice a hoarse whisper.

"She took me aside and told me this was what it had all been for...to snare a rich husband, to have the world at my monied fingertips. She'd accomplished her goal and I should be grateful to her for the years she'd dedicated to me, all that she'd sacrificed in order that I would have what my beauty declared that I deserved."

"You...you didn't marry him," Taylor said in the form of a statement rather than a question. "No."

"Oh, yes, of course I did," she said, her hands clutched tightly in her lap. "Legally I was a woman. Emotionally? I was a child, who wasn't capable of defying my mother in any way. And in the back of my mind there was this tiny seed of hope that it just might be possible that Walter wanted me, *me the person,* not just the outer shell I presented."

"What...what happened?"

"It was a sham, a cruel joke." Janice laughed, a sharp bark of bitter sound laced with threatening tears. "I was a trophy to Walter, a doll he could dress up in expensive clothes and even more expensive jewelry, then show off in public, strutting his stuff as he displayed his prize.

"At home? He ignored me beyond the bedroom. If we weren't having sex, I was to sit pretty, like a beautiful marionette, until such time as he wanted to parade me in public again."

Taylor muttered an earthy expletive and his hands curled into tight fists on his thighs.

"When I was twenty, Walter went away for the weekend, which was a common occurrence. He disappeared quite frequently without a word of where he was going, or when he'd be back. But that time? He *never* returned. He was having an affair with my mother, you see. They'd been drinking heavily, Walter lost control of the car and they slammed into a tree. They were killed instantly.

"I waited for the tears to come, the grief, the sense of loss, but they never came. All I felt was free. For the first time in my entire life I was free to be *me*. I was a wealthy widow. There was nothing standing in the way of my own dreams. Nothing, I soon discovered when I went to college, except my damnable beauty."

"So you diminished it as much as possible," Taylor said quietly.

"Yes. I reverted to my maiden name and became the invisible woman, who no one ever looked at twice. I created a facade that brought me peace and contentment. There would be no man who would want me as I now presented myself, but I didn't trust anyone to see past the beauty if I put it on display. But then?"

Tears filled Janice's eyes and she struggled to retain control of her emotions.

"Then you, Taylor. I thought at first that I was a challenge to you, a mystery of sorts, something to relieve the boredom of your fast-lane, single-scene life. But time went on and you stayed with me. You were so caring, so tender.

"Then...then you said that you loved me, *me*, just as I was. Accepted me, just as I was. Oh, I was so happy. So very happy."

Two tears spilled onto Janice's pale cheeks and she wiped them away with jerky motions, her hands shaking.

"But it was all a cruel lie," she whispered, a sob catching in her throat. "Another sham. You'd been embarrassed long enough by being seen with me in public. It was time to decorate the ugly duckling. No, no, it was time to awaken Sleeping Beauty, transform me into what you wanted me to be."

Taylor lunged to his feet. "No! You've got it all wrong, Janice, I swear it."

"There is the evidence!" She pointed at the silver box. "Damn you, Taylor Sinclair. Outer appearance is just as important to you as it was to my mother, to Walter, as it is to society at large. *You want me to be beautiful.*"

"No. Yes." Taylor dragged one hand through his hair. "But not for me, Janice, for you."

"Stop it," she said, covering her ears with her hands. "I won't listen to any more of your lies." She dropped her hands, got to her feet and moved behind the chair, gripping the top of it tightly. "Go away, Taylor. Just go away and leave me alone."

"No, I can't, not like this. Janice, our entire future is at stake here. I love you, want to marry you, spend the rest of my life by your side."

Janice shook her head, unable to stop the flow of tears that streamed down her face and along her neck.

"Listen to me. Please, please, listen to me," Taylor said, his voice raspy with emotion. "I told you that I was afraid of loving, saw it as guaranteed heartbreak. To love was to lose that love, by death, or divorce.

"I was struggling with that belief, and I fought it, finally conquered that terror. I came to realize that the risk was worth it if I was with you."

He took a shuddering breath.

"Brandon made me face the truth of what I was doing. A last shadow of fear kept me from encouraging you to be true to yourself as a woman. I couldn't lose you to another man, if no man looked twice at you. I was so selfish, so damn wrong, to be doing what I did to you."

Taylor stared up at the ceiling for a long moment in an attempt to gain control of his emotions, then he looked at Janice again.

"I love you, Janice. I love you enough to risk losing you. I love you enough to want you to be free to be who you really are. The gift I sent you was my way of declaring that truth. I never meant to hurt you. What I did by giving you the dress, the makeover certificate, I did for you. I don't care about outer appearances, I swear I don't. Do you believe me? Do you, Janice?"

Janice said one word in a voice filled with tears of sorrow, a voice echoing the sound of her shattering heart, a voice that sliced through Taylor like the blade of a sharp knife.

One word.

"No."

Every muscle in Taylor's body tightened as the realization hit him that he was losing, at that very moment, the only woman he had ever loved. He felt stripped bare, helpless.

It was over.

Tears of heartache and soul-deep despair filled his eyes.

Forcing himself to place one foot in front of the other, he made his way to the door, then opened it to reveal a dark, empty night that waited to swallow him up into a pit of chilling, black loneliness.

He hesitated, pleading silently with Janice to tell him not to go, to tell him she believed him, trusted him, loved him as he loved her.

Silence beat against him like angry, painful fists.

He stumbled from the house, closing the door with a quiet click.

Janice sank to the floor behind the chair, covered her face with her hands and wept.

Janice hardly remembered the remaining hours of the weekend as she barely functioned in a tear-filled haze of misery.

On Monday morning she was exhausted, having been only able to doze fitfully before waking again to relive that final scene with Taylor.

She opened the closet in her bedroom to reach

for one of her regulation suits, then her hand stilled. She crossed the room and sank onto the edge of the bed.

What was the point in hiding her beauty? she thought. The camouflage had served no purpose. She'd been betrayed in the end anyway. Lied to. Manipulated. Trusted her heart to a man who had smashed it to smithereens.

She lifted her chin and squared her shoulders.

"No more tears," she said aloud. "No more. And no more ugly clothes. I'm going to be me, who I really am from this day forward. I'm going to be true to myself. Yes. Wake up, Sleeping Beauty, this is the first day of the rest of your life. Alone. One hummingbird. Not two together. One. Fine."

Tears threatened and she jumped to her feet, refusing to give way to them.

When she left the house to go to the boutique, she was wearing trim white slacks and a red silk blouse. Her hair was a golden cloud tumbling down her back.

That evening she went next door to Shirley's, and in a rush of words poured out the tale of what had happened with Taylor. Before Shirley could express her sympathies, Janice grabbed her friend's hand and said they were going shopping for a new wardrobe for Janice Jennings, the woman she now was and intended to remain.

The next day, Janice had her hair trimmed, leaving it long but cut into a more fashionable and flat-tering style. She purchased makeup that suited her taste, applying just enough to enhance her features.

During the following days, Janice slowly became accustomed to, and began to enjoy, the compliments she received on her appearance. She produced genuine smiles as she said "Thank you."

Her new clothes started to feel as though they actually belonged to her, and she found herself looking forward to putting together an attractive ensemble each morning.

She was Janice Jennings and she was beautiful, she repeated in her mind like a mantra. Yes, that was fine, just fine.

And through it all she missed Taylor, ached for Taylor, couldn't stop the flow of tears during the long, lonely nights without Taylor Sinclair.

On the eighteenth day since her dreams of a future with Taylor had ended, Janice was extremely busy at Sleeping Beauty, attempting to assist five women at once with their selections.

She was wearing a pale pink, gauze peasant dress that was nipped in at her tiny waist by a gauze belt, and scooped low to the edges of her shoulders. The material swung as she moved, affording a glimpse of her long, shapely legs and the womanly slope of her hips.

She was standing behind the counter, placing a satin teddy into a tissue-lined box when the door to the shop opened yet again.

Janice glanced up, then did a double take, her eyes widening, her heart racing.

Taylor was there. But...but this was not a Taylor she had ever seen before.

He was wearing a slightly wrinkled, white dress shirt, black slacks that were several inches too short, white socks and brown shoes.

His hair was slicked down and parted in the middle. Clutched in one of his hands was a soggy paper towel wrapped around several wilting pink carnations.

Taylor was there, she thought incredulously, and he looked absolutely horrible.

"Janice Jennings," Taylor boomed from where he stood in the center of the store.

Every woman in the boutique stopped and stared at the strange-looking man who was loudly demanding Janice's attention.

"Janice Jennings," Taylor repeated. "I love you. I will always love you. I'm asking you to be my wife, my soul mate, the mother of my children."

One of the women dissolved into a fit of laughter.

"He's got to be kidding," she said to the friend next to her, but loud enough for all to hear. "Janice is gorgeous. She'd never make a commitment to a geek like that. Oh, this is hysterically funny."

"He could be quite handsome if he tried," her friend said. "But...good grief, he's just awful."

"I realize I'm not much to look at, Janice," Taylor went on. "But outer appearances aren't important, are they? Not to me. Not to you. Are they, Janice?''

"You bet your sweet bippy they are," another woman said. "No offense, young man, but you are way out of your league. Janice is one of the beautiful people and you, dear boy, are not. And, oh, yes, that is, indeed, important."

"Janice," Taylor shouted. "Will you marry me? Will you? Please?"

Janice took a much-needed breath, only then realizing she'd stopped breathing.

Taylor loved her, truly loved her, her heart sang. He hadn't lied to her. Everything he'd said that fateful night in her living room had been true, spoken from his heart and soul.

This ridiculous and endearing performance he was putting on was declaring to the world, for all to see, that outer appearances meant nothing to him. He loved her, *her*, just as she loved him.

"Janice?" Taylor said.

She ran around the counter, across the floor and into Taylor's arms, nearly toppling him over.

"Yes," she said, smiling through tears of joy. "Yes, I'll marry you. Oh, Taylor, thank you for loving me enough to show me you honestly understand, truly love me for who I am, not what I look like."

"Thank God," Taylor said, wrapping his arms around her as he dropped his meager bouquet to the floor. "Ah, Janice, I've missed you so much. I love you so damn much."

"And I love you."

"Is this a happy ending or something?" one woman said to another.

"I guess," the other woman replied with a shrug. "They certainly are an...unusual-looking couple. Oh, well, love is blind, as the saying goes."

"No," Taylor said quietly, close to Janice's lips. "Love sees beyond the trimmings, the outside packaging."

"Yes," Janice whispered. "And love has the power and wisdom to awaken Sleeping Beauty."

Taylor captured Janice's mouth in a kiss that sealed their commitment to forever.

They were two hummingbirds united, oblivious to the applause produced by the women in the boutique.

They were Janice and Taylor...together.

EPILOGUE

They were married a week later in judge's chambers with Clem, Mary Alice and Shirley as witnesses.

The bride was stunningly beautiful in a lovely peach-colored suit and a short veil. The groom was devastatingly handsome in a dark suit, white shirt and a peach-colored tie.

The ceremony was repeated that afternoon in the charming gazebo on the town square in Prescott, with Taylor's lifelong friends in attendance.

The next several days were a flurry of activity as they made arrangements for their respective businesses so they could leave on a two-week honeymoon cruise.

On the morning they were to catch a plane to fly

to California to board the cruise ship, Taylor announced that he had to stop at his office on the way to the airport.

"Did you forget to do something?" Janice said as they drove away from the house.

"Not exactly," Taylor said. "I just need to take care of some unfinished business."

In the parking lot, Taylor removed a tissue-wrapped package from the back seat of the car. Janice looked at him questioningly, but he only smiled as they went into the building.

In Taylor's office, he pushed aside the cracked pen set from the edge of his desk and removed the tissue from the mysterious parcel in his hand.

Then carefully, reverently, he set a framed picture in the empty space on the desk. It was a color photograph of him and Janice taken in the gazebo in Prescott on their wedding day.

"There," he said, pulling Janice into his arms. "Now everything is perfect, Mrs. Sinclair."

"Yes," she said softly, gazing up at him. "Everything is perfect, Mr. Sinclair, and it will be…forever."

* * * * *

In August 1999, find out what secrets
bachelor Ben Rizzoli harbors when
bestselling author Joan Elliott Pickart's
miniseries, THE BACHELOR BET
continues with THE MOST ELIGIBLE M.D.,
Special Edition #1262.

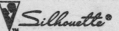

Available July 1999 from Silhouette Books...

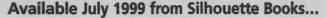

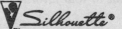

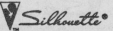

This August 1999, the legend
continues in Jacobsville

DIANA PALMER

LOVE WITH A
LONG, TALL TEXAN

A trio of brand-new short stories featuring
three irresistible Long, Tall Texans

GUY FENTON, LUKE CRAIG
and CHRISTOPHER DEVERELL...

This August 1999, Silhouette brings readers an
extra-special collection for Diana Palmer's legions
of fans. Diana spins three unforgettable stories of
love—Texas-style! Featuring the men you can't get
enough of from the wonderful town of Jacobsville,
this collection is a treasure for all fans!

They grow 'em tall in the saddle in Jacobsville—and
they're the best-looking, sweetest-talking men to be
found in the entire Lone Star state. They are proud,
hardworking men of steel and it will take
the perfect woman to melt their hearts!

Don't miss this collection of original
Long, Tall Texans stories...available in
August 1999 at your favorite retail outlet.